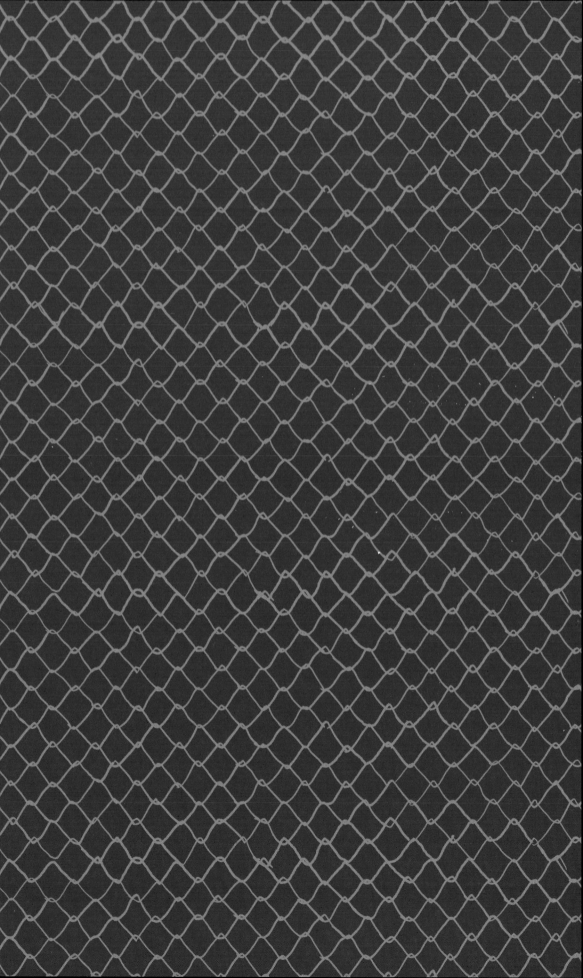

Epigram

Whenever I find myself growing grim about the mouth;
whenever it is a damp, drizzly November in my soul;
whenever I find myself involuntarily pausing before coffin warehouses,
and bringing up the rear of every funeral I meet;
and especially when my hypos get such an upper hand of me,
that it requires a strong moral principle to prevent me
from deliberately stepping into the street,
and methodically knocking people's hats off —

Then, I account it high time to get to sea as soon as I can.

Herman Melville
MOBY DICK (1851)

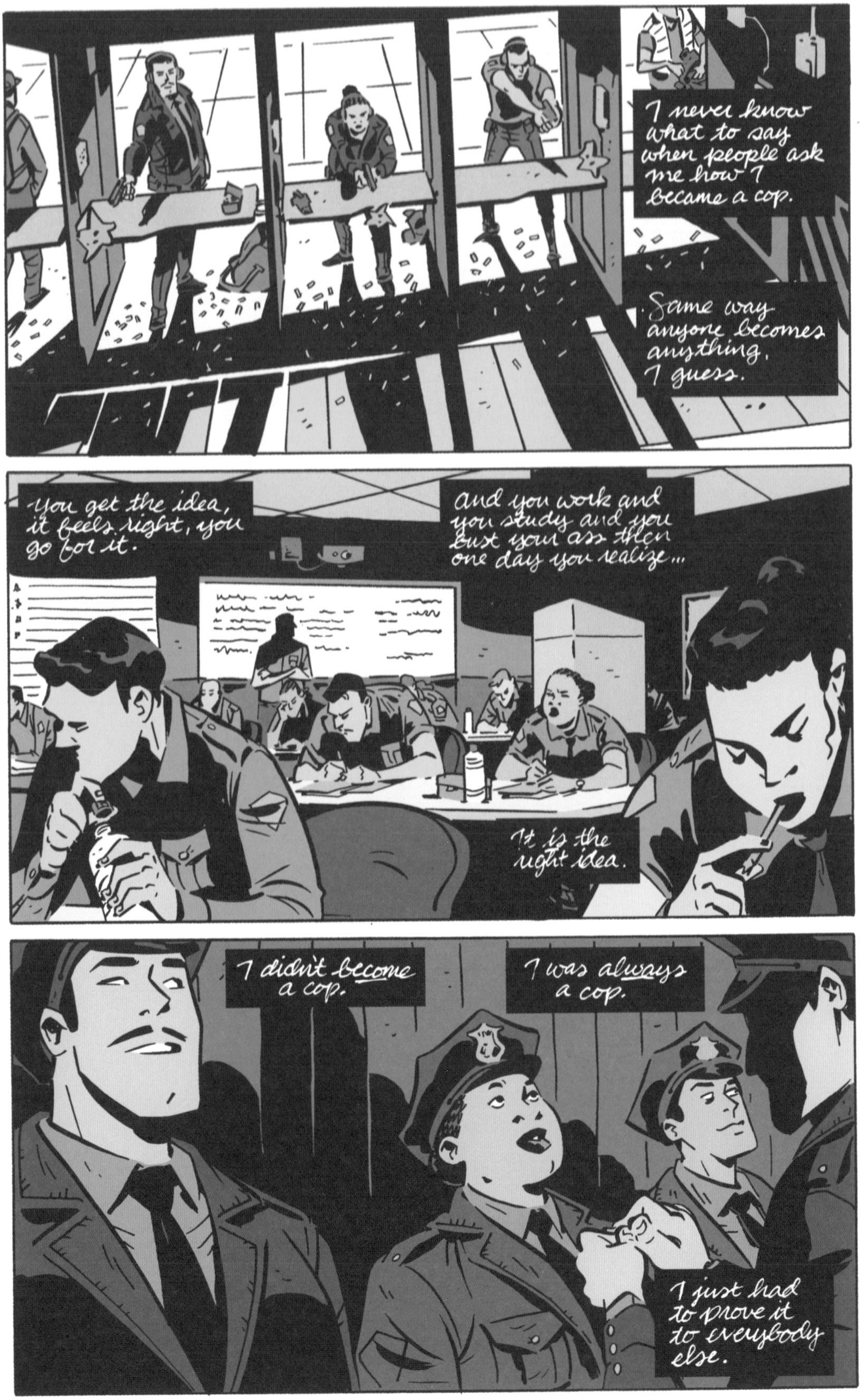
I never know what to say when people ask me how I became a cop.
Same way anyone becomes anything, I guess.
You get the idea, it feels right, you go for it.
And you work and you study and you bust your ass then one day you realize...
It is the right idea.
I didn't become a cop.
I was always a cop.
I just had to prove it to everybody else.

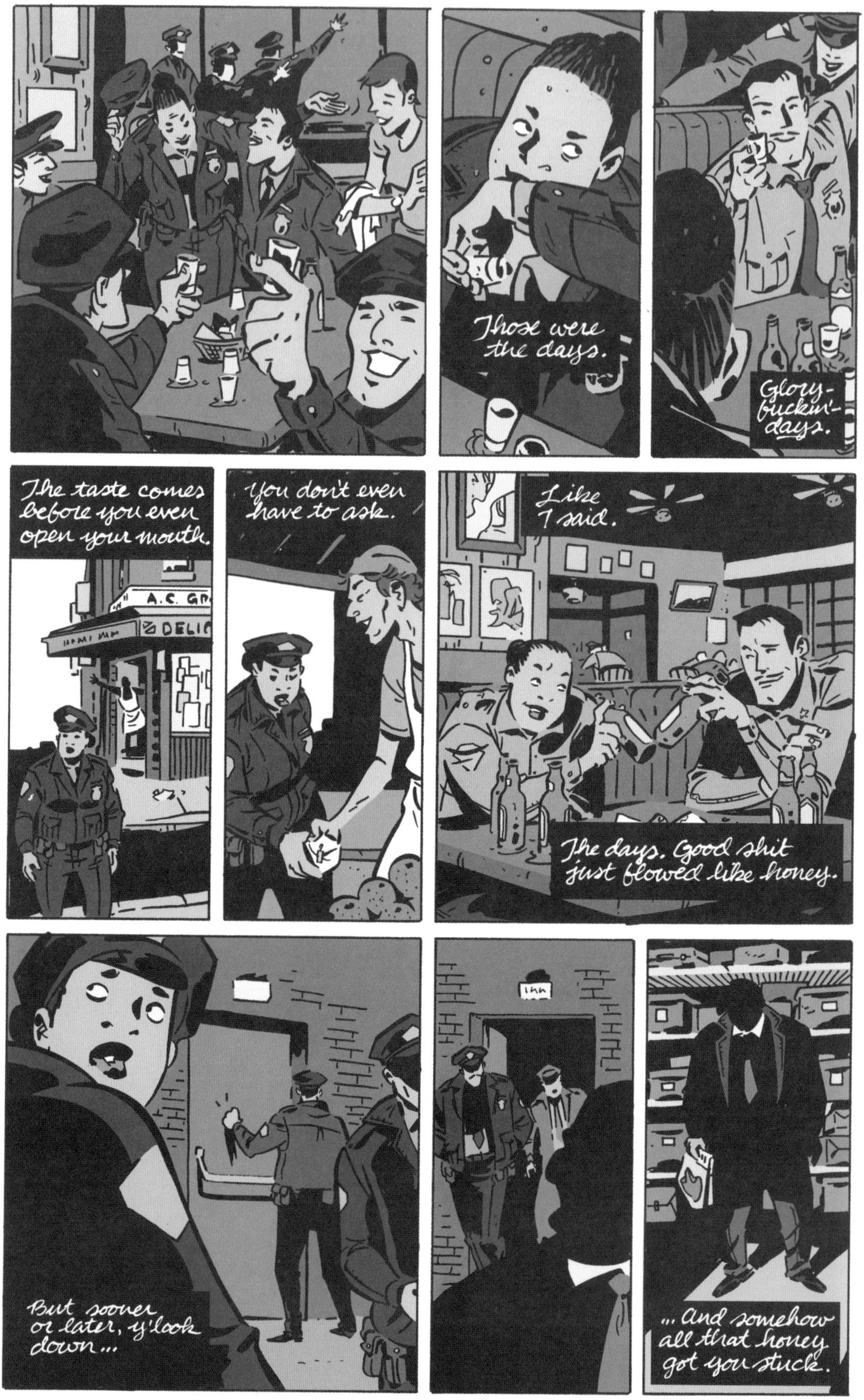

Those were the days.
Glory-fuckin'-days.
The taste comes before you even open your mouth.
A.C. GR
DELI
You don't even have to ask.
Like I said.
The days. Good shit just flowed like honey.
But sooner or later, y'look down...
... And somehow all that honey got you stuck.

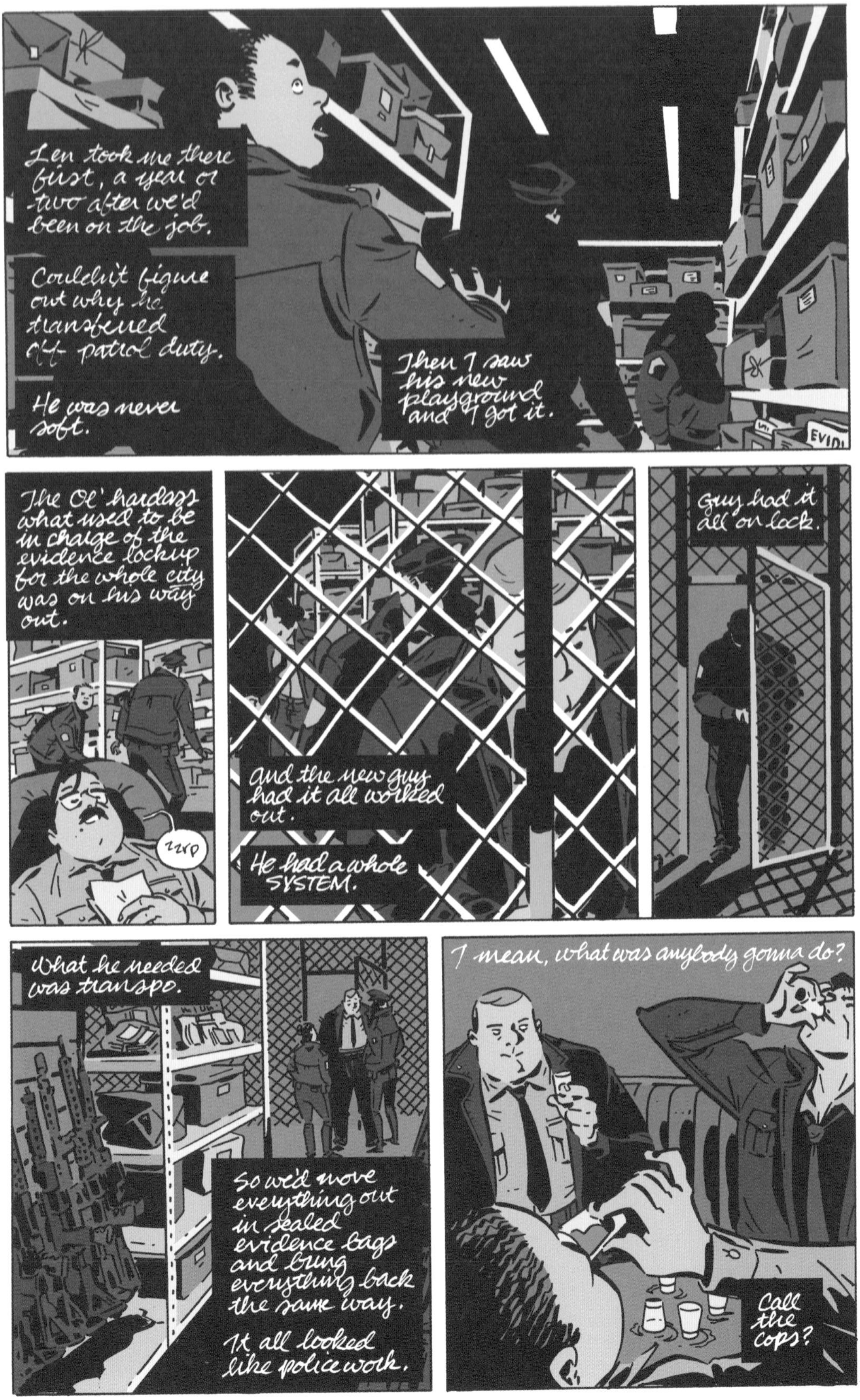
Len took me there first, a year or two after we'd been on the job.
Couldn't figure out why he transferred off patrol duty.
He was never soft.
Then I saw his new playground and I got it.
EVID
The Ol' hardass what used to be in charge of the evidence lockup for the whole city was on his way out.
zzrp
And the new guy had it all worked out.
He had a whole SYSTEM.
Guy had it all on lock.
What he needed was transpo.
So we'd move everything out in sealed evidence bags and bring everything back the same way.
It all looked like police work.
I mean, what was anybody gonna do?
Call the cops?

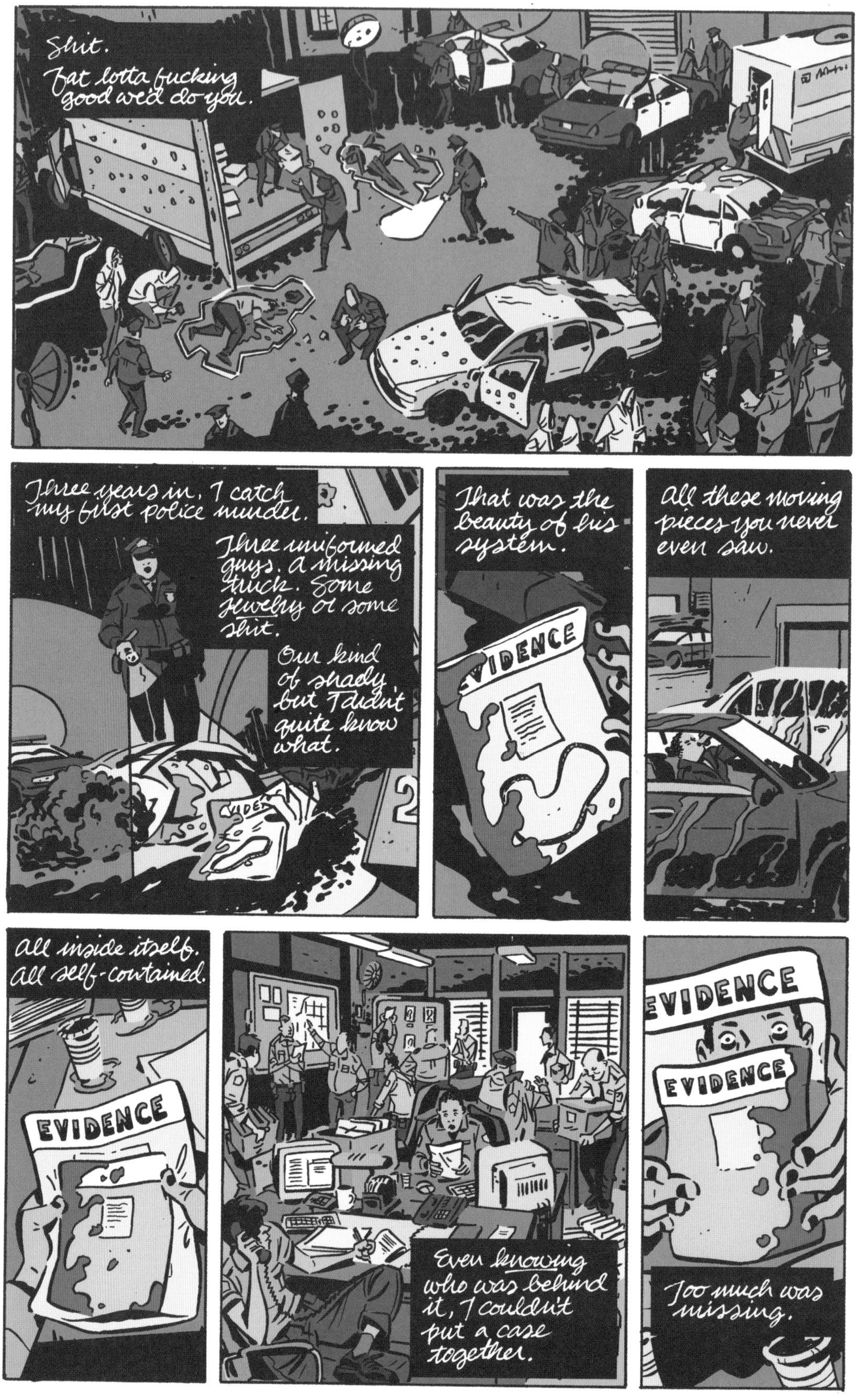
Shit.
Fat lotta fucking good we'd do you.
Three years in, I catch my first police murder.
Three uniformed guys. A missing truck. Some jewelry or some shit.
Our kind of shady but I didn't quite know what.
That was the beauty of his system.
All these moving pieces you never even saw.
EVIDENCE
All inside itself. All self-contained.
EVIDENCE
Even knowing who was behind it, I couldn't put a case together.
EVIDENCE
EVIDENCE
Too much was missing.

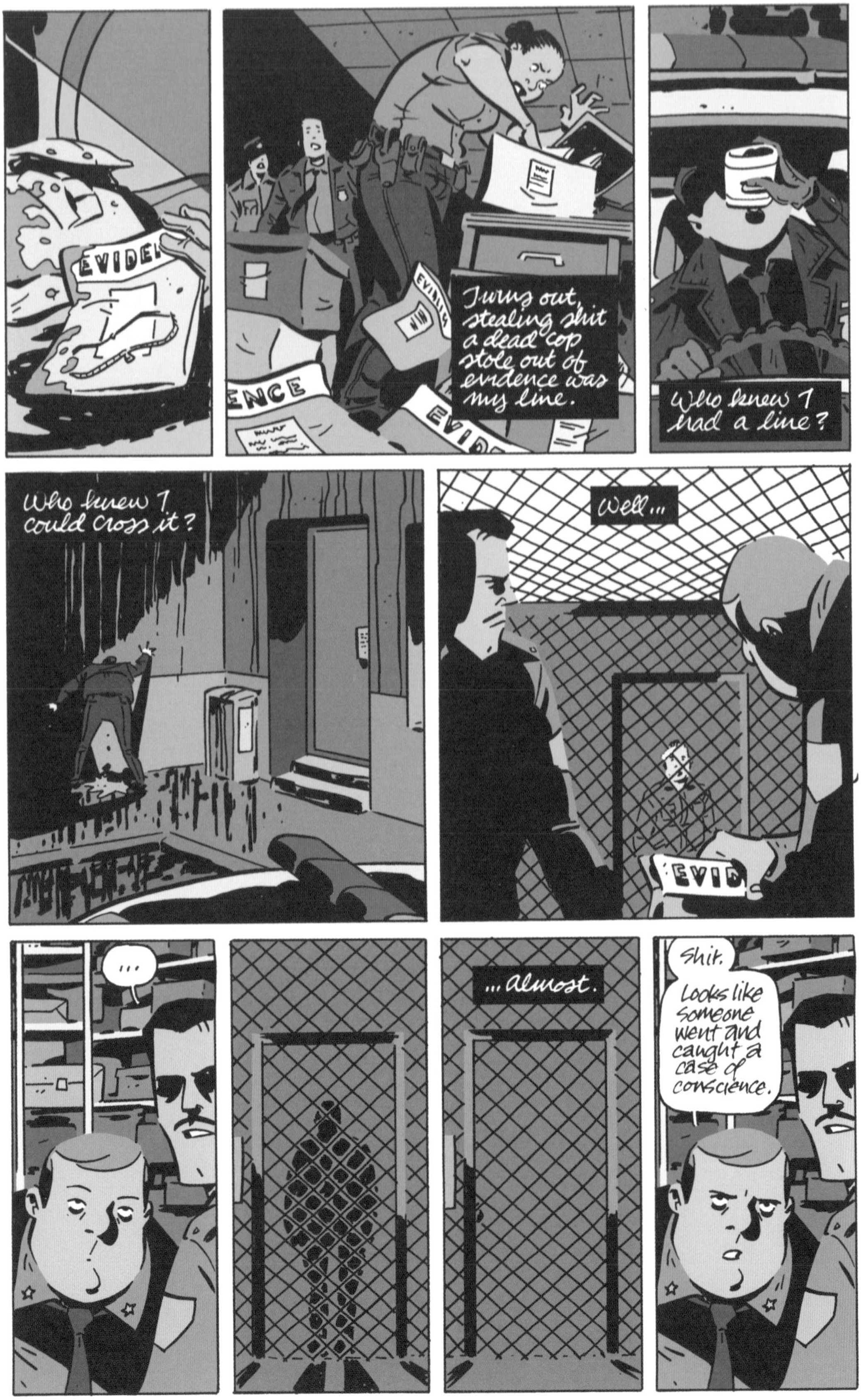
EVIDE
Turns out, stealing shit a dead cop stole out of evidence was my line.
EVIDENCE
ENCE
EVID
Who knew I had a line?
Who knew I could cross it?
Well...
EVID
...
...almost.
Shit.
Looks like someone went and caught a case of conscience.

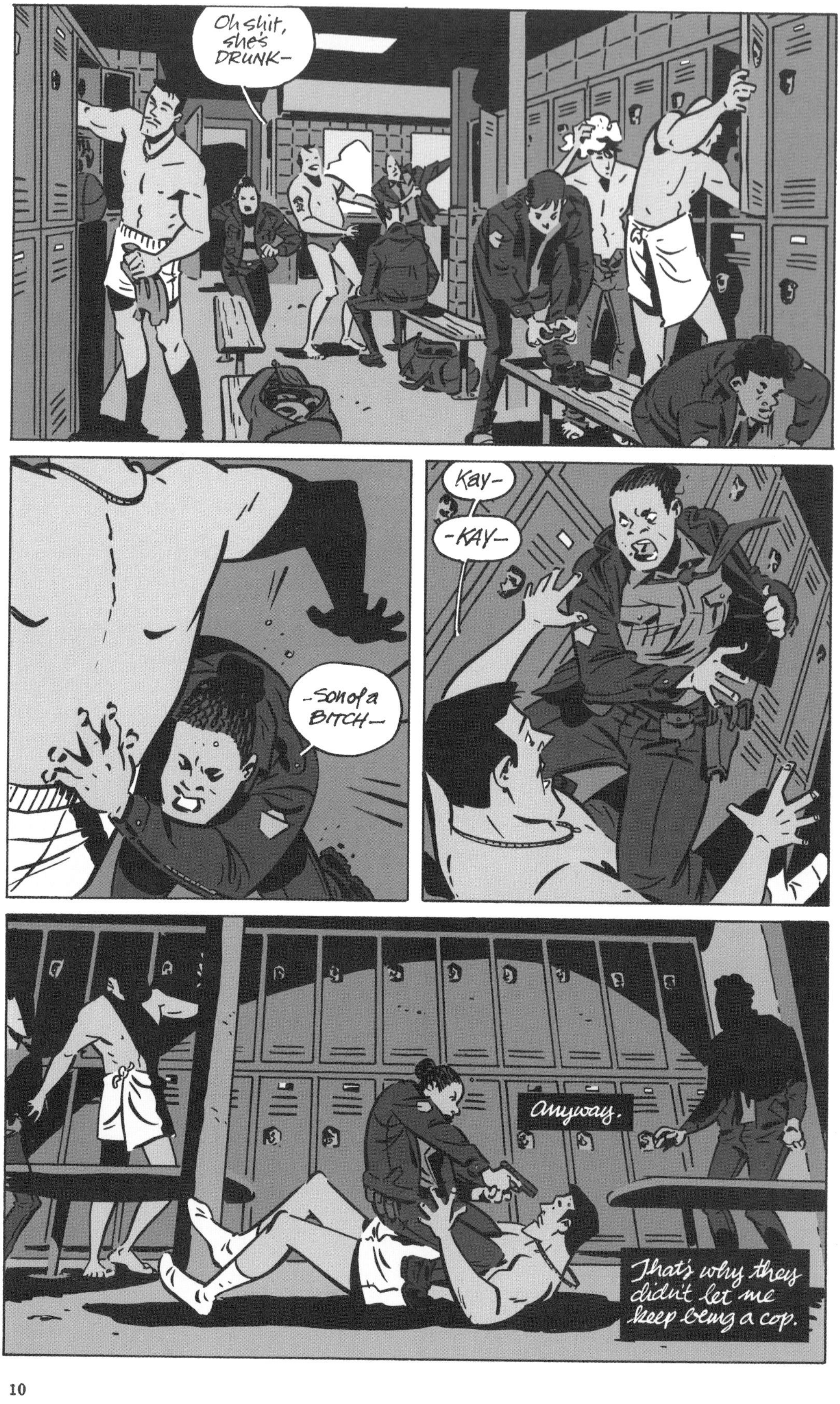
Oh shit, she's DRUNK-
-Son of a BITCH-
Kay-
-KAY-
anyway.
That's why they didn't let me keep being a cop.

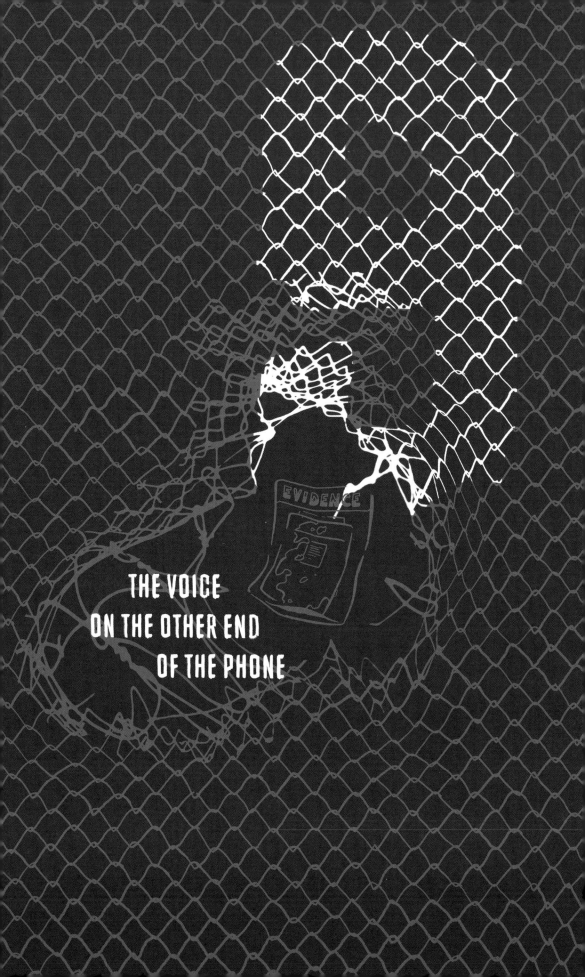

THE VOICE
ON THE OTHER END
OF THE PHONE

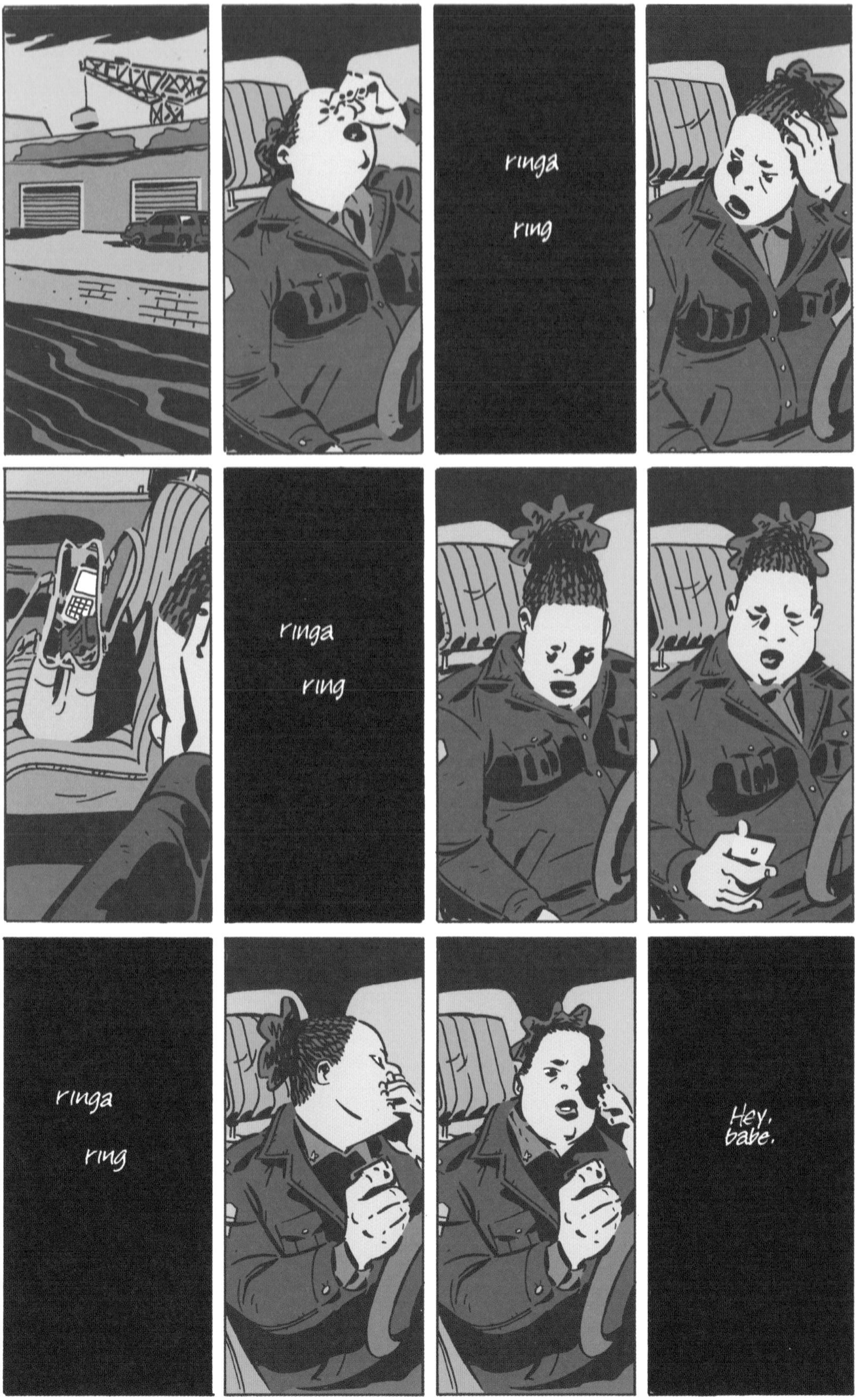
ringa
ring
ringa
ring
ringa
ring
Hey, babe.

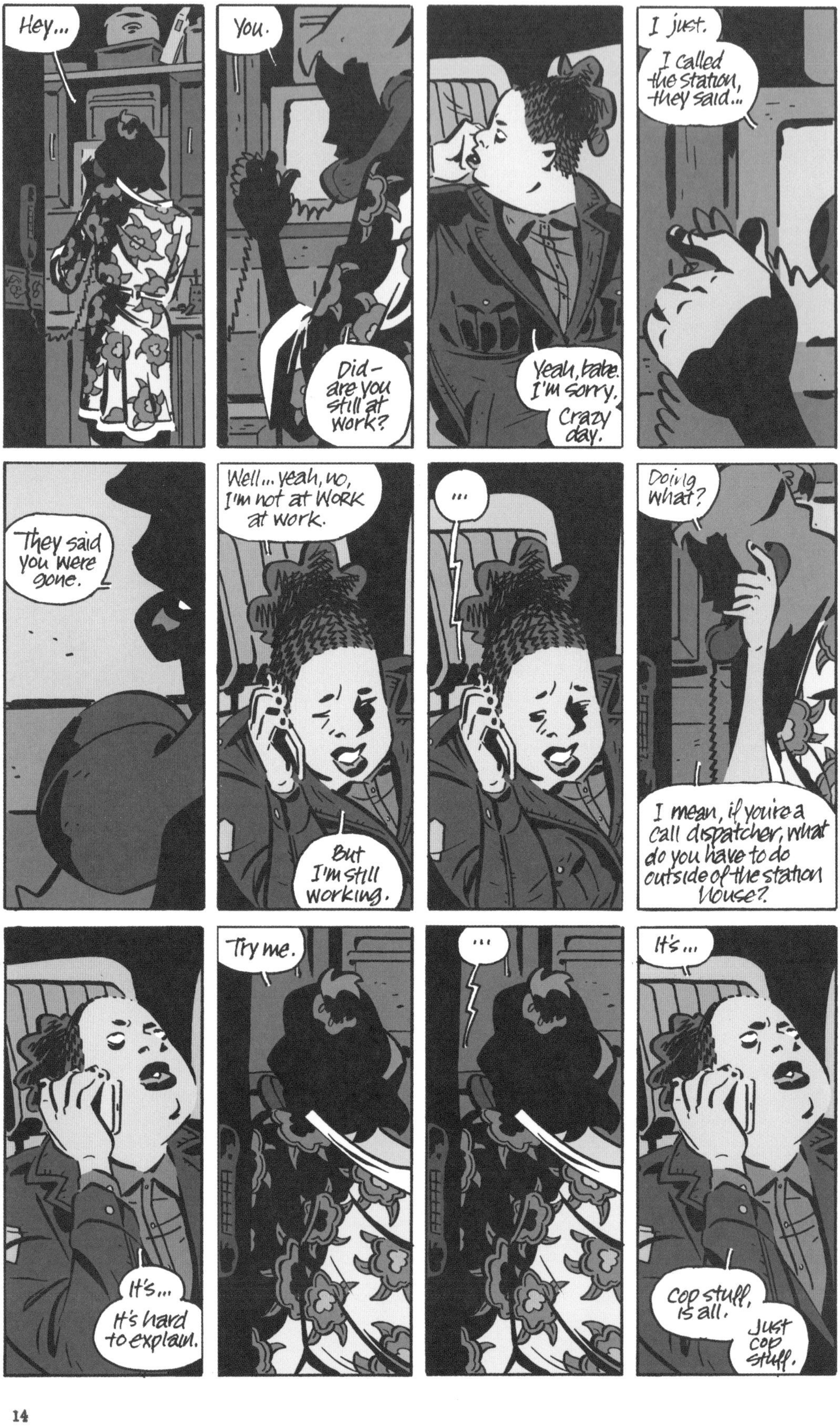
Hey...
You.
Did- are you still at work?
Yeah, babe. I'm sorry.
Crazy day.
I just.
I called the station, they said...
They said you were gone.
Well... yeah, no, I'm not at WORK at work.
But I'm still working.
...
Doing what?
I mean, if you're a call dispatcher, what do you have to do outside of the station house?
It's...
It's hard to explain.
Try me.
...
It's...
Cop stuff, is all.
Just cop stuff.

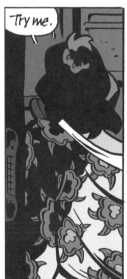

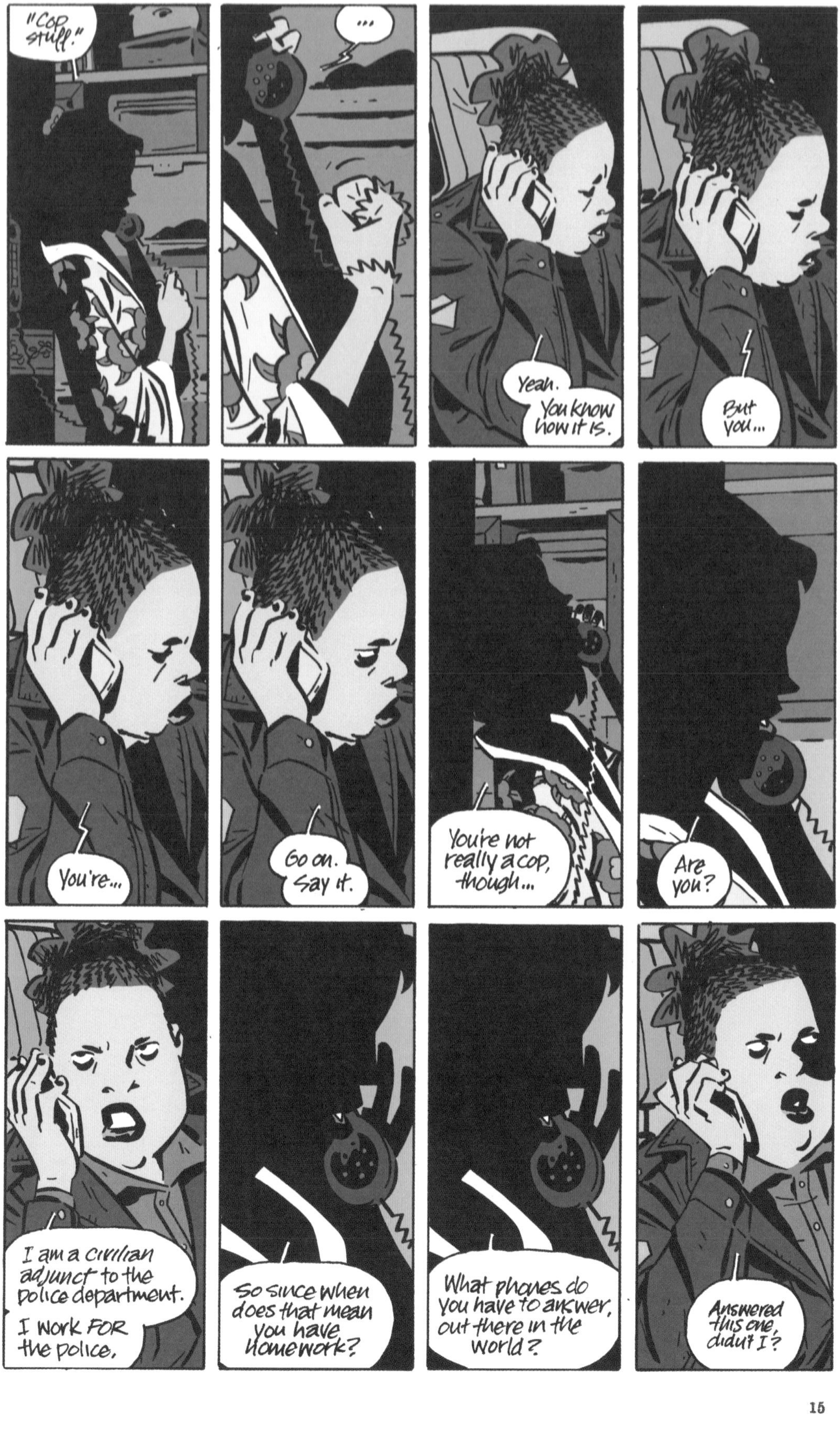
"Cop stuff."
...
Yeah. You know how it is.
But you...
You're...
Go on. Say it.
You're not really a cop, though...
Are you?
I am a civilian adjunct to the police department.
I work FOR the police.
So since when does that mean you have homework?
What phones do you have to answer, out there in the world?
Answered this one, didn't I?

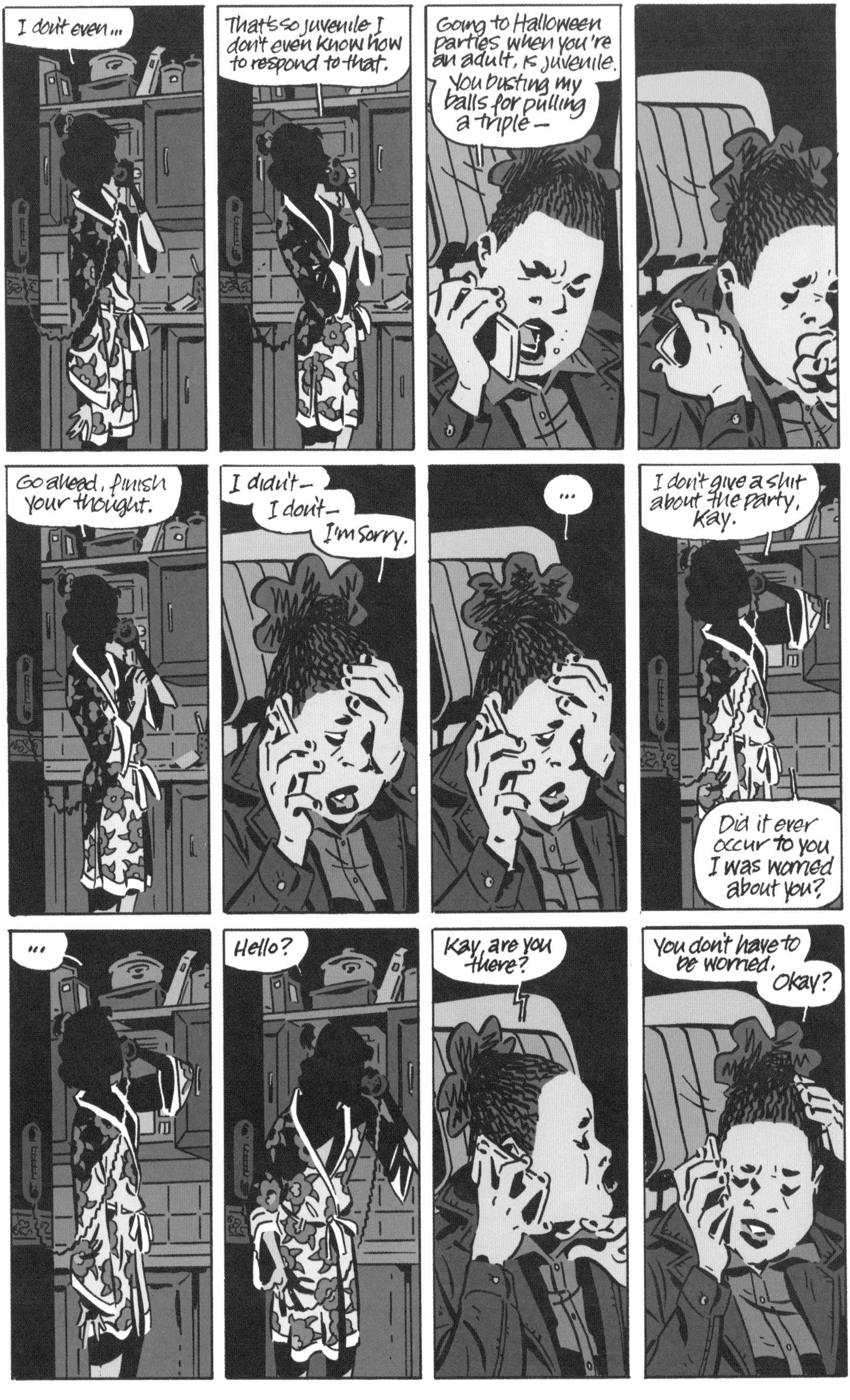
I don't even...
That's so juvenile I don't even know how to respond to that.
Going to Halloween parties when you're an adult, is juvenile.
You busting my balls for pulling a triple—
Go ahead, finish your thought.
I didn't—
I don't—
I'm sorry.
...
I don't give a shit about the party, Kay.
Did it ever occur to you I was worried about you?
...
Hello?
Kay, are you there?
You don't have to be worried.
Okay?

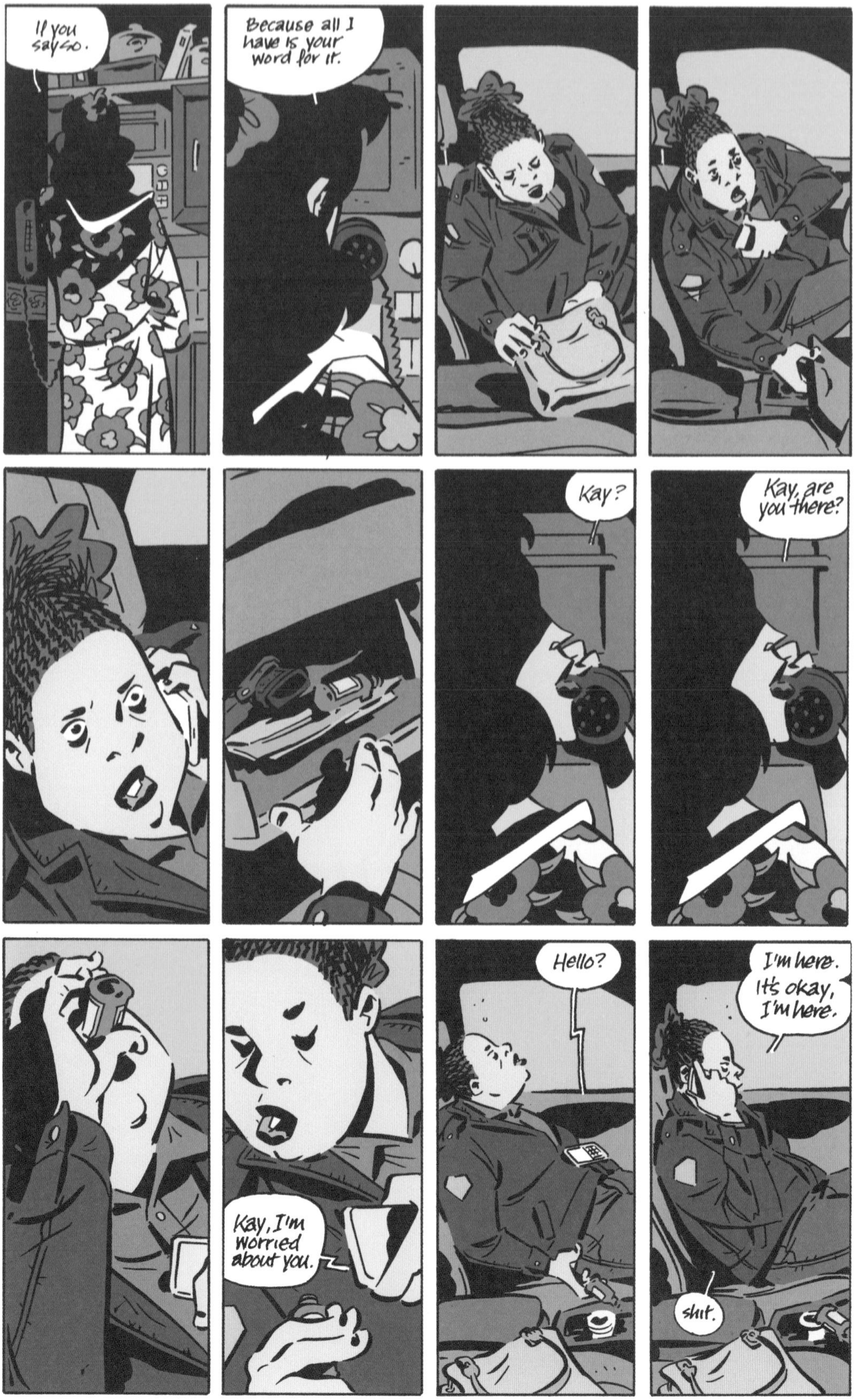
If you say so.
Because all I have is your word for it.
Kay?
Kay, are you there?
Kay, I'm worried about you.
Hello?
I'm here. It's okay, I'm here.
shit.

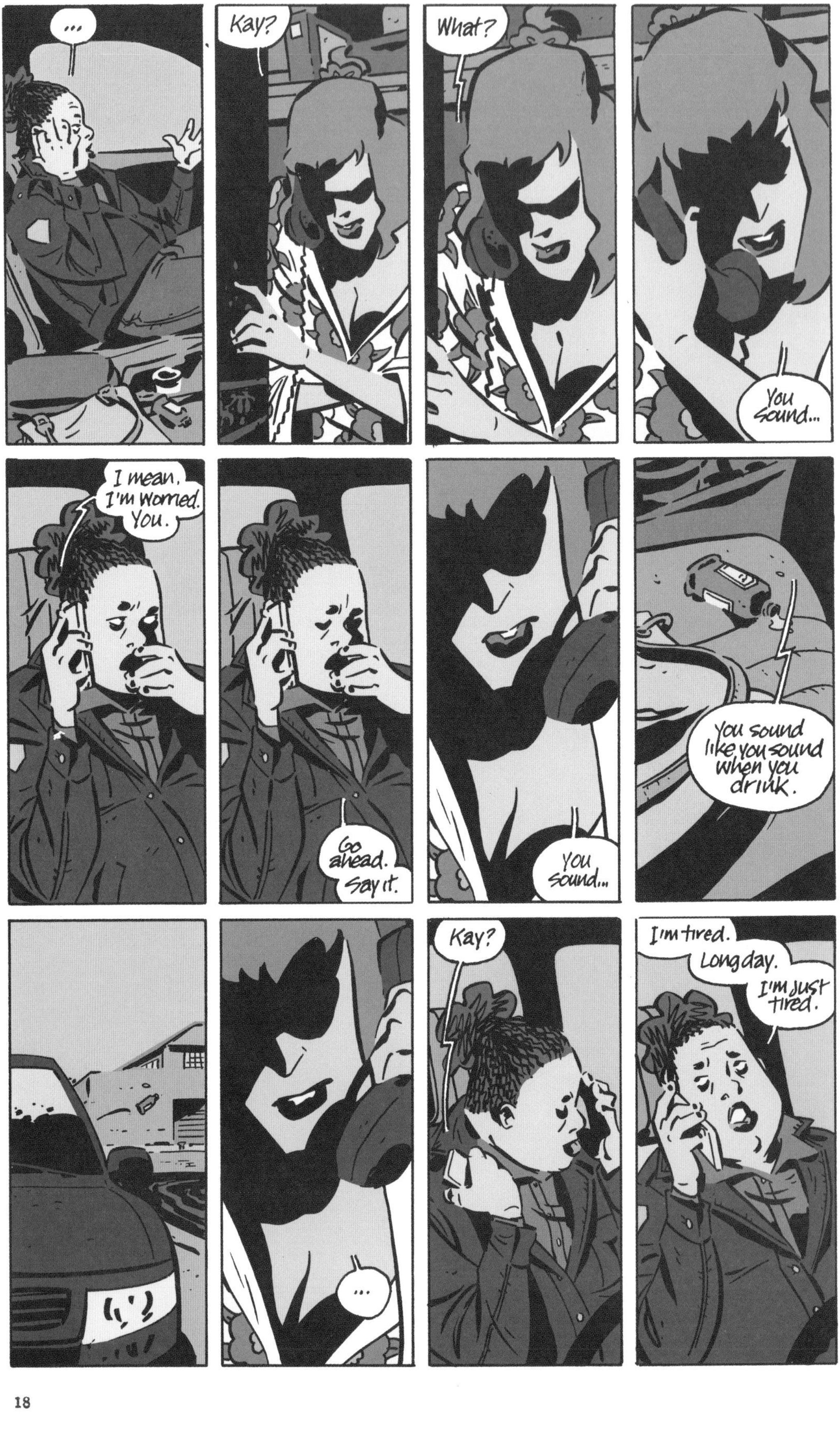
...
Kay?
What?
You sound...
I mean. I'm worried. You.
Go ahead. Say it.
You sound...
You sound like you sound when you drink.
...
Kay?
I'm tired.
Long day.
I'm just tired.

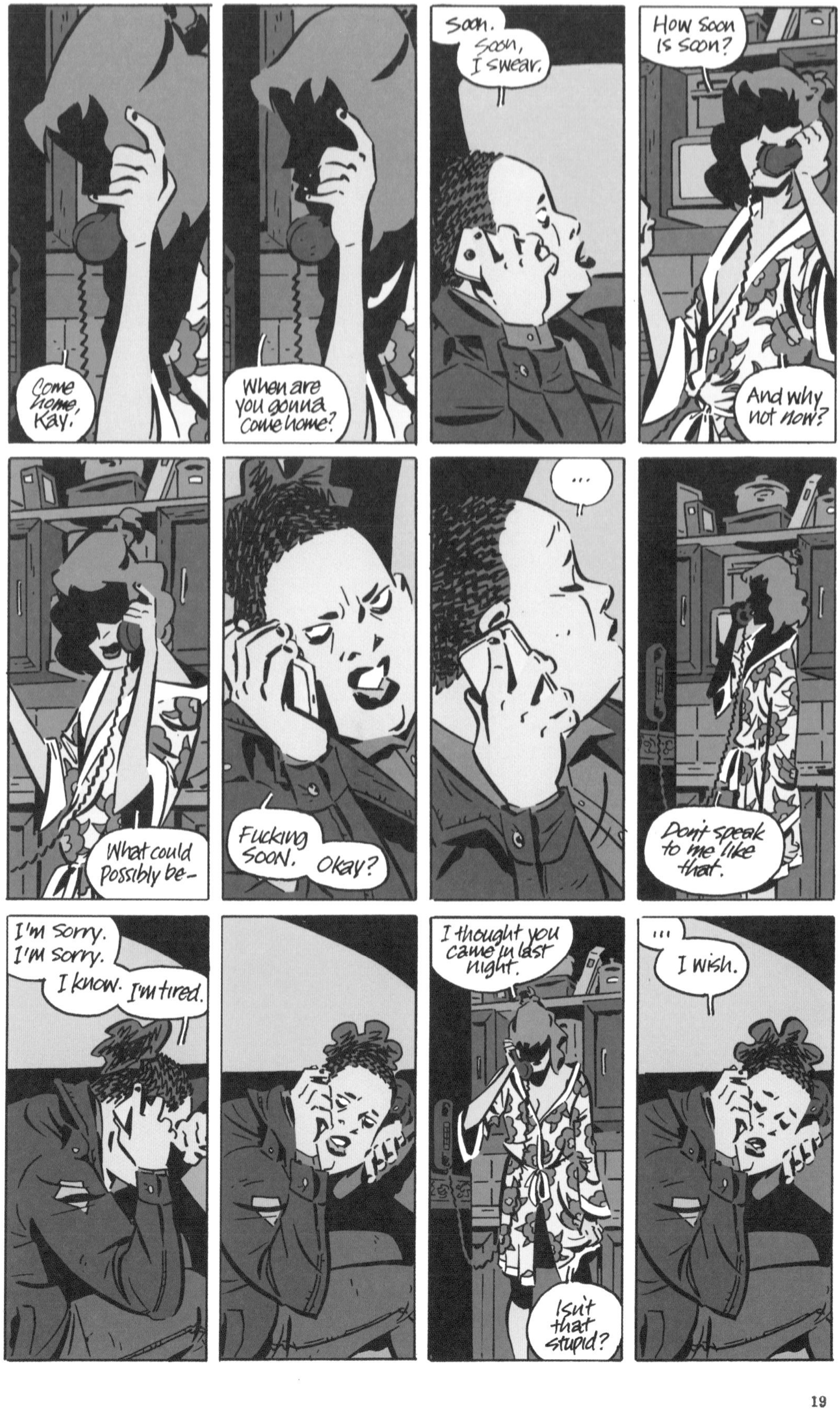
Come home, Kay.
When are you gonna come home?
Soon. Soon, I swear.
How soon is soon?
And why not now?
What could possibly be-
Fucking soon.
Okay?
...
Don't speak to me like that.
I'm sorry. I'm sorry.
I know.
I'm tired.
I thought you came in last night.
Isn't that stupid?
...
I wish.

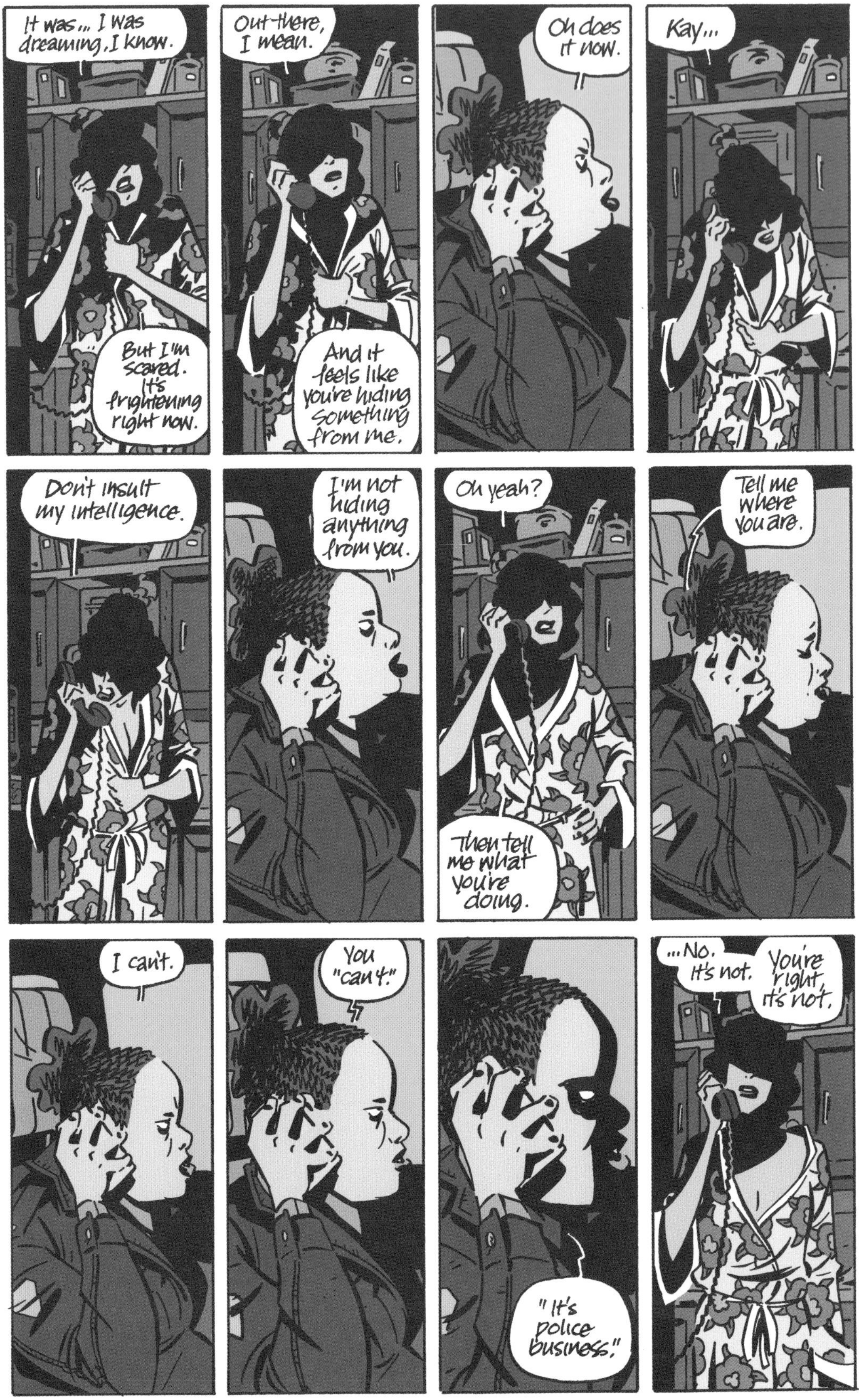
It was... I was dreaming, I know.
But I'm scared. It's frightening right now.
Out there, I mean.
And it feels like you're hiding something from me.
Oh does it now.
Kay...
Don't insult my intelligence.
I'm not hiding anything from you.
Oh yeah?
Then tell me what you're doing.
Tell me where you are.
I can't.
You "can't."
"It's police business."
...No. It's not.
You're right, it's not.

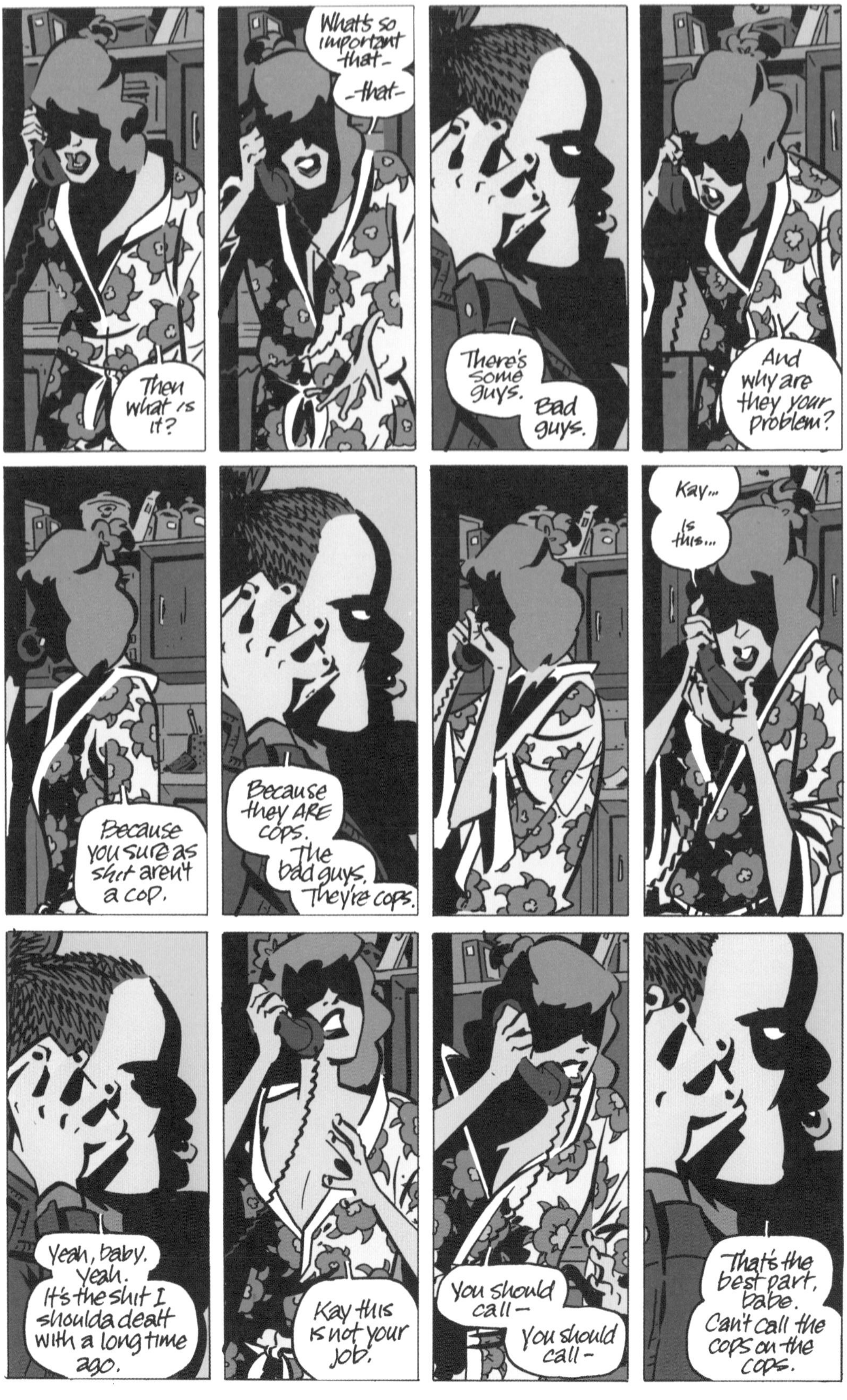
Then what is it?
What's so important that-
-that-
There's some guys.
Bad guys.
And why are they your problem?
Because you sure as shit aren't a cop.
Because they ARE cops.
The bad guys. They're cops.
Kay...
is this...
Yeah, baby. Yeah. It's the shit I shoulda dealt with a long time ago.
Kay this is not your job.
You should call-
You should call-
That's the best part, babe. Can't call the cops on the cops.

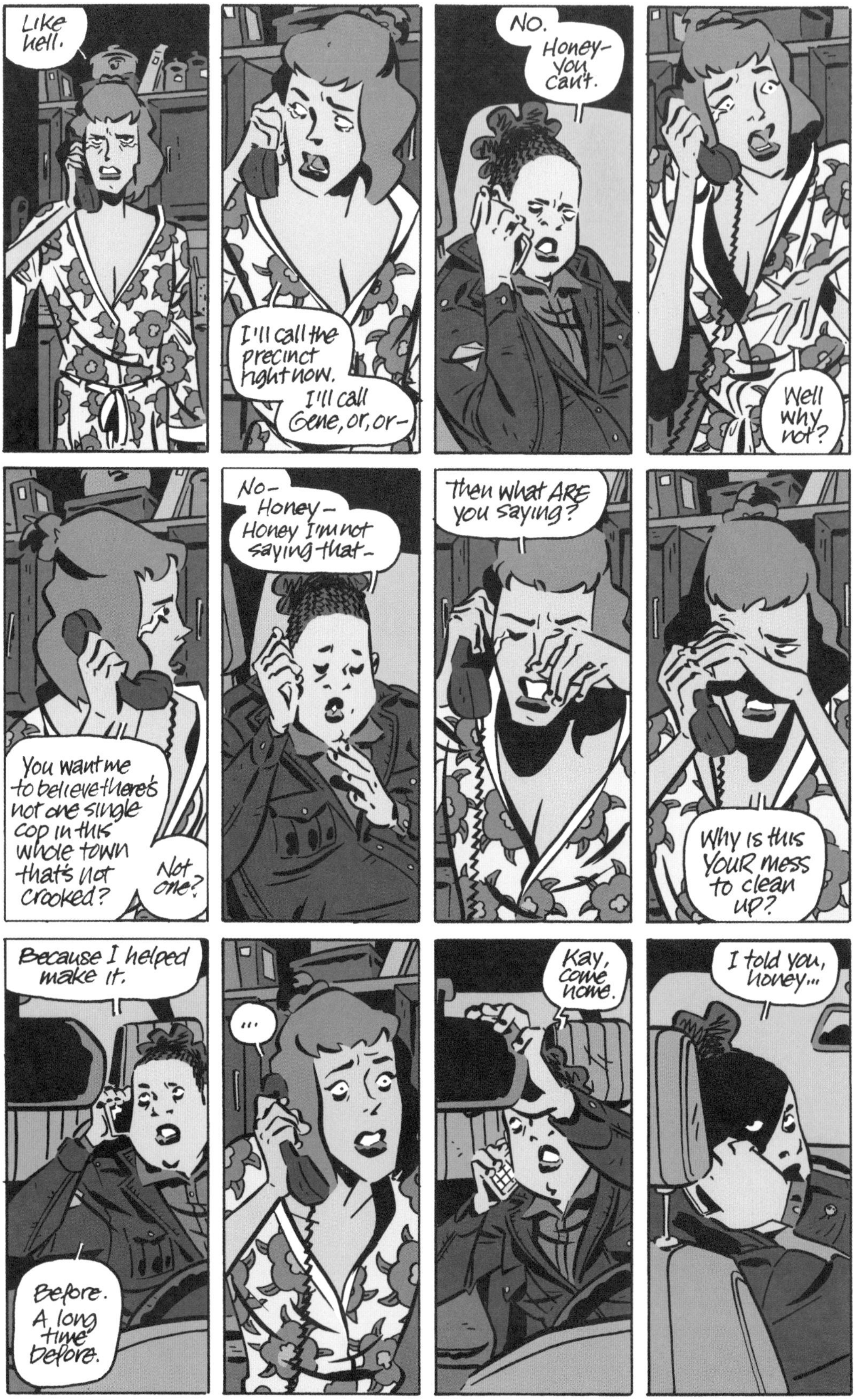
Like hell.
I'll call the precinct right now.
I'll call Gene, or, or–
No.
Honey– You can't.
Well why not?
You want me to believe there's not one single cop in this whole town that's not crooked?
Not one?
No– Honey– Honey I'm not saying that–
Then what ARE you saying?
Why is this YOUR mess to clean up?
Because I helped make it.
Before. A long time before.
...
Kay, come home.
I told you, honey...

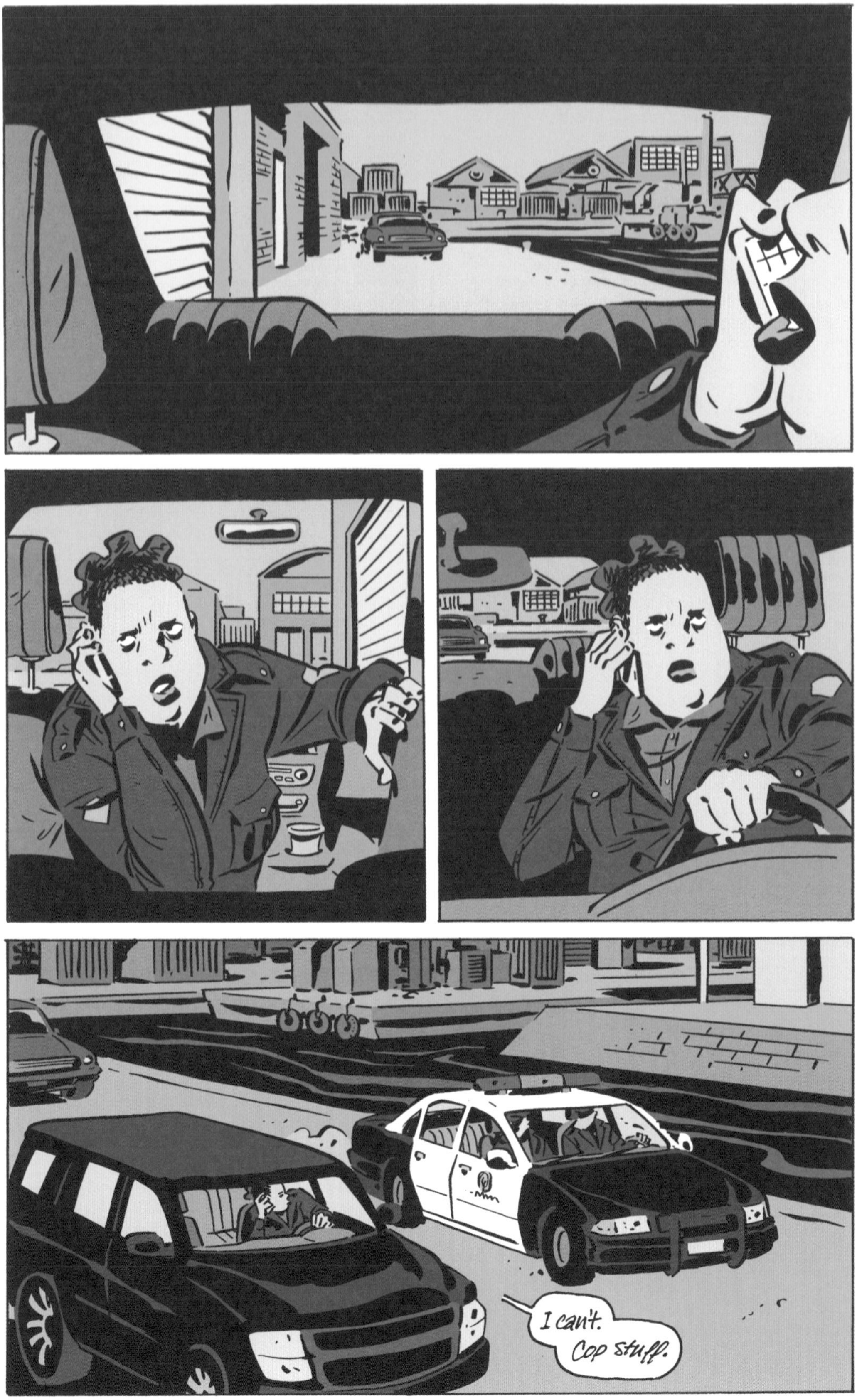
I can't.
Cop stuff.

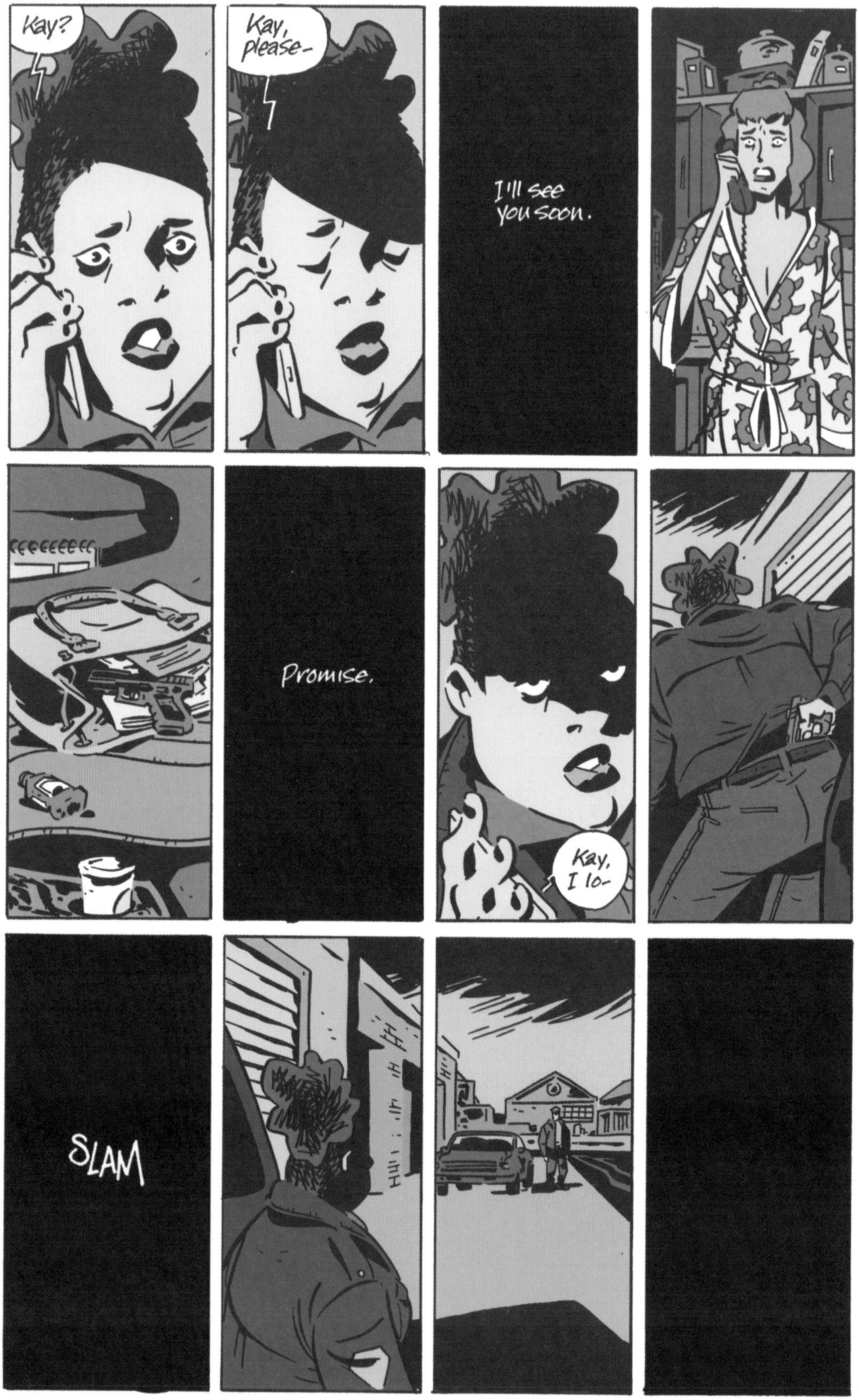
Kay?
Kay, please-
I'll see you soon.
Promise.
Kay, I lo-
SLAM

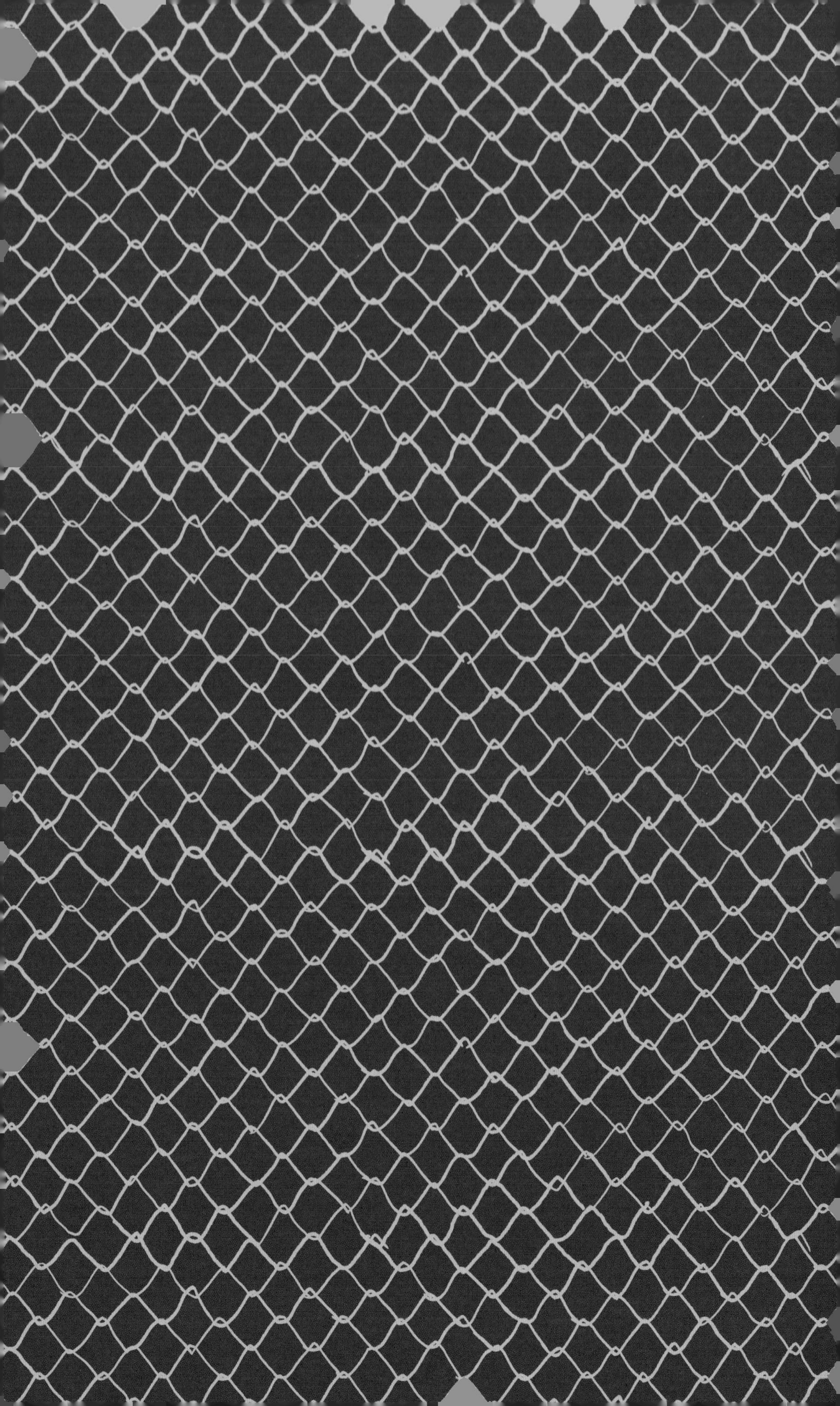

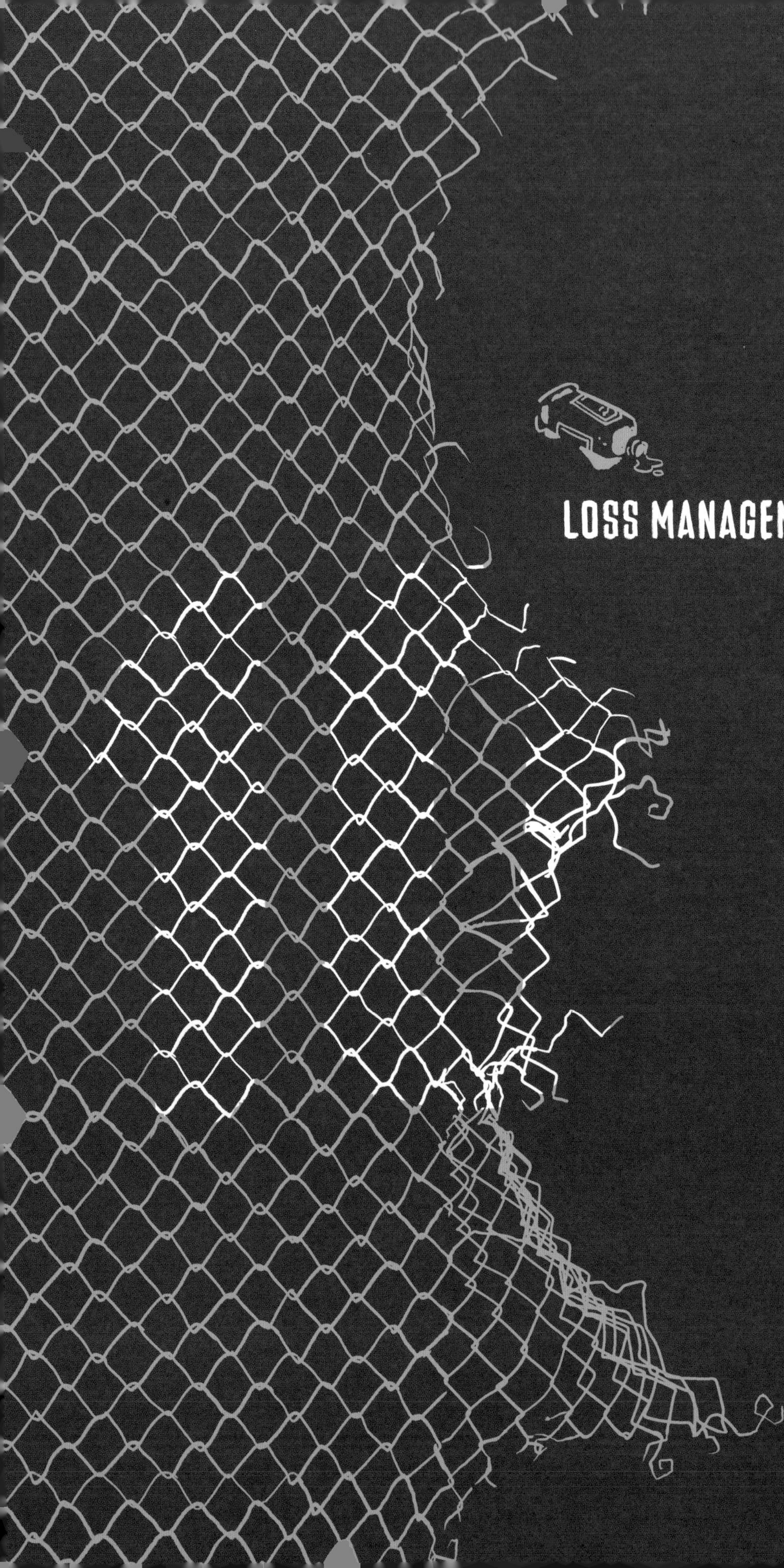

LOSS MANAGEMENT

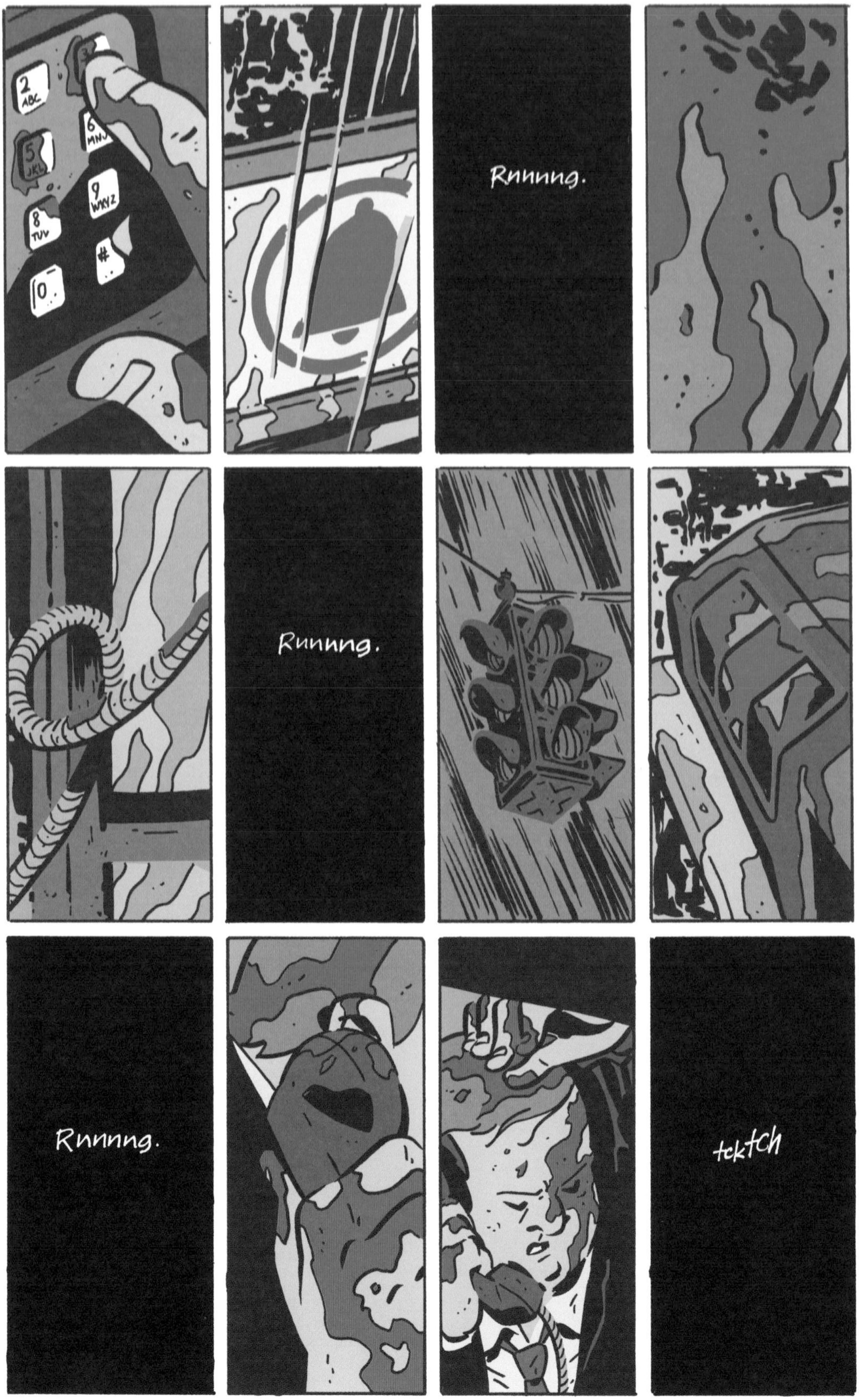
2 ABC
6 MNO
5 JKL
9 WXYZ
8 TUV
#
0
Rnnnng.
Rnnnng.
Rnnnng.
tcktch

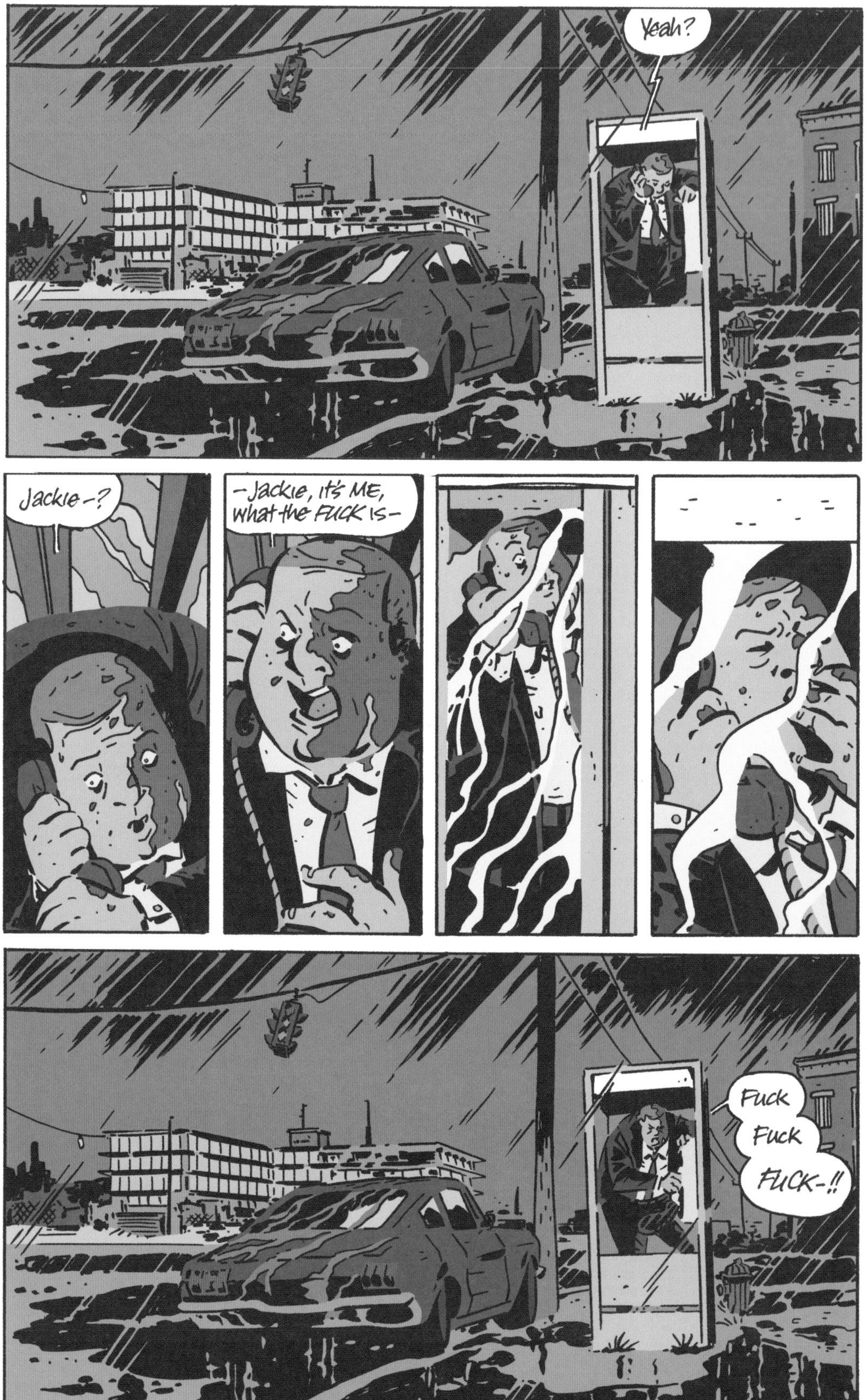
Yeah?
Jackie-?
-Jackie, it's ME, what the FUCK is-
Fuck
Fuck
FUCK-!!

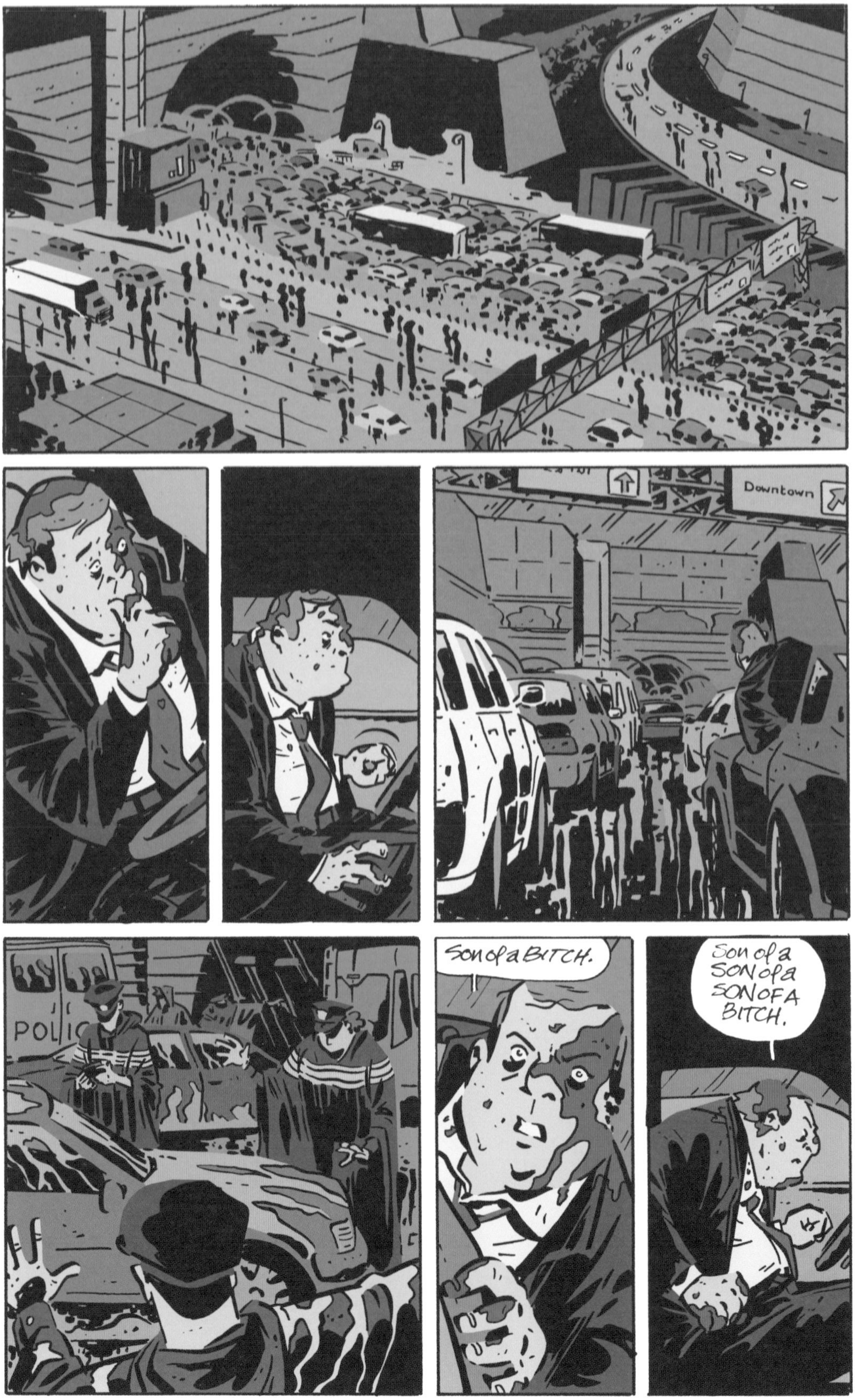
Downtown
POLIC
SON of a BITCH.
Son of a
SON of a
SON OF A
BITCH.

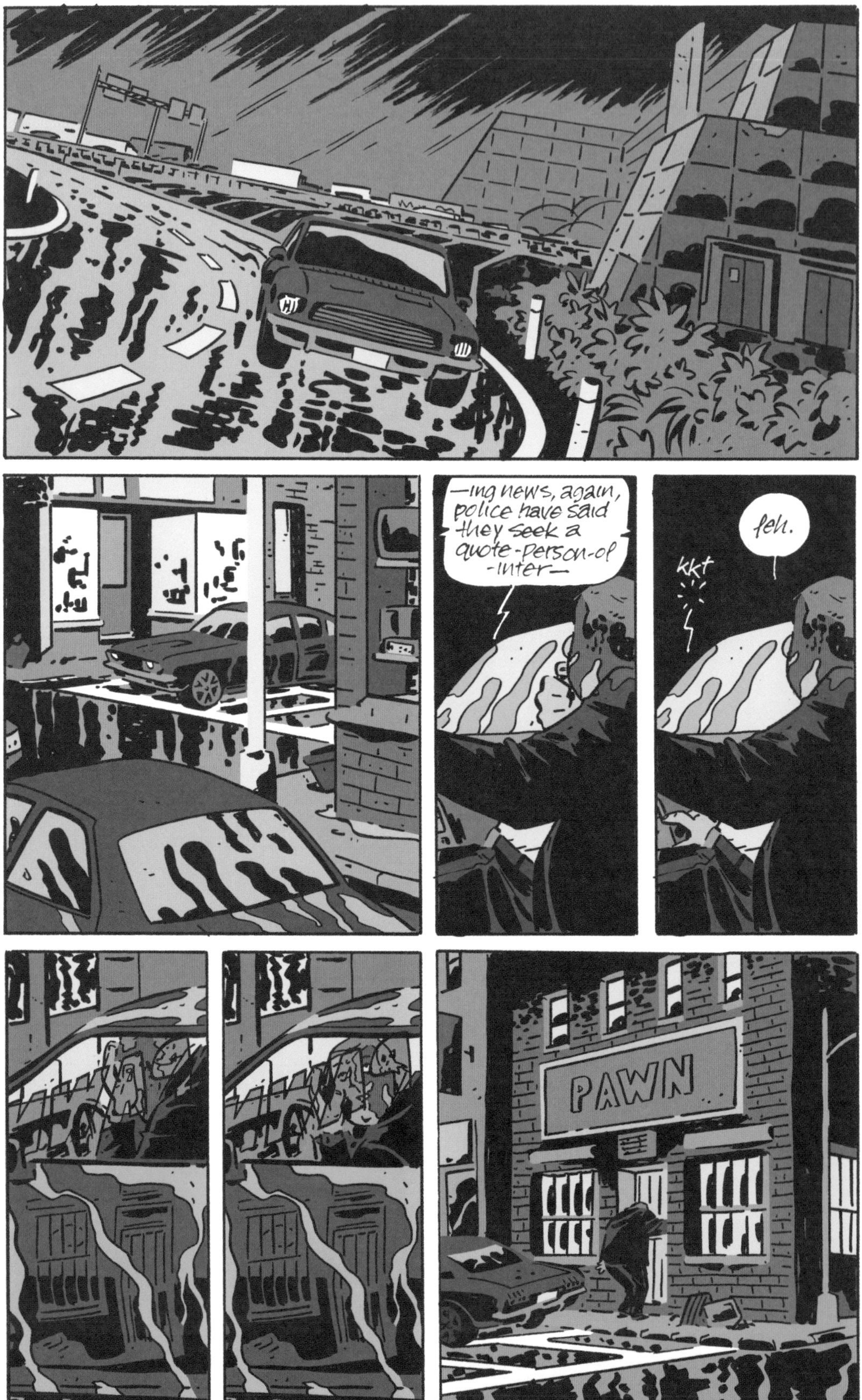
—ing news, again, police have said they seek a quote-person-of -inter—
kkt
feh.
PAWN

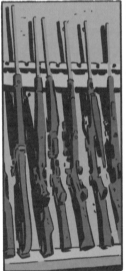

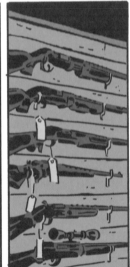

Can I take a look at the .44?

What is that, that gold. Like a hip hop thing?

Damned if I know, I just buy and sell 'em.

Well if it works, who cares, right?

Yeah something like that.

Say, pal, you look like hell.

Eh. You should see the other guy.

How much?

18, plus the filing and background check fees, that brings it to 20. Half-down puts it on hold for you during the waiting period.

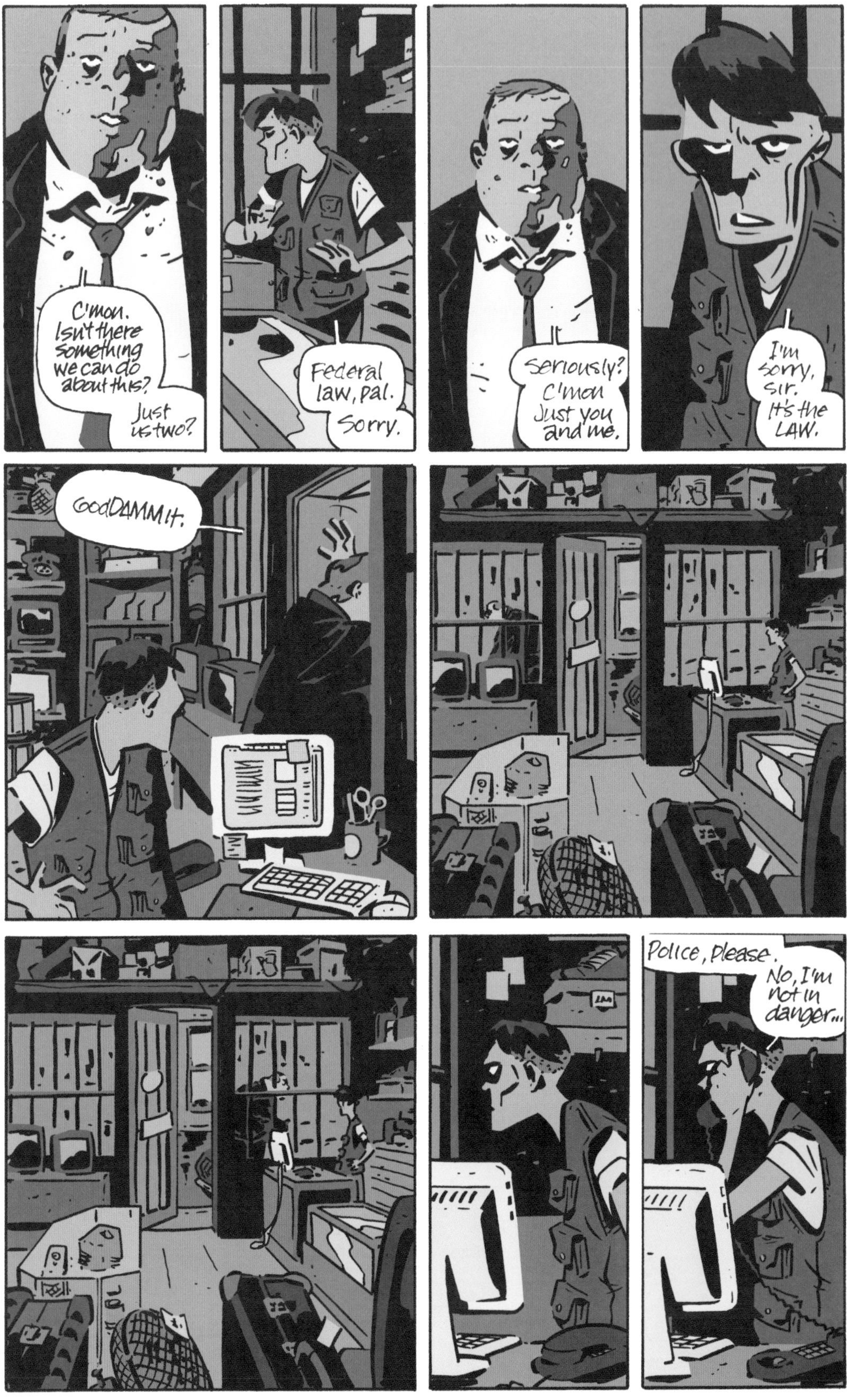
C'mon. Isn't there something we can do about this?
Just us two?
Federal law, pal.
Sorry.
Seriously? C'mon
Just you and me.
I'm sorry, sir. It's the LAW.
GodDAMMit.
Police, please.
No, I'm not in danger...

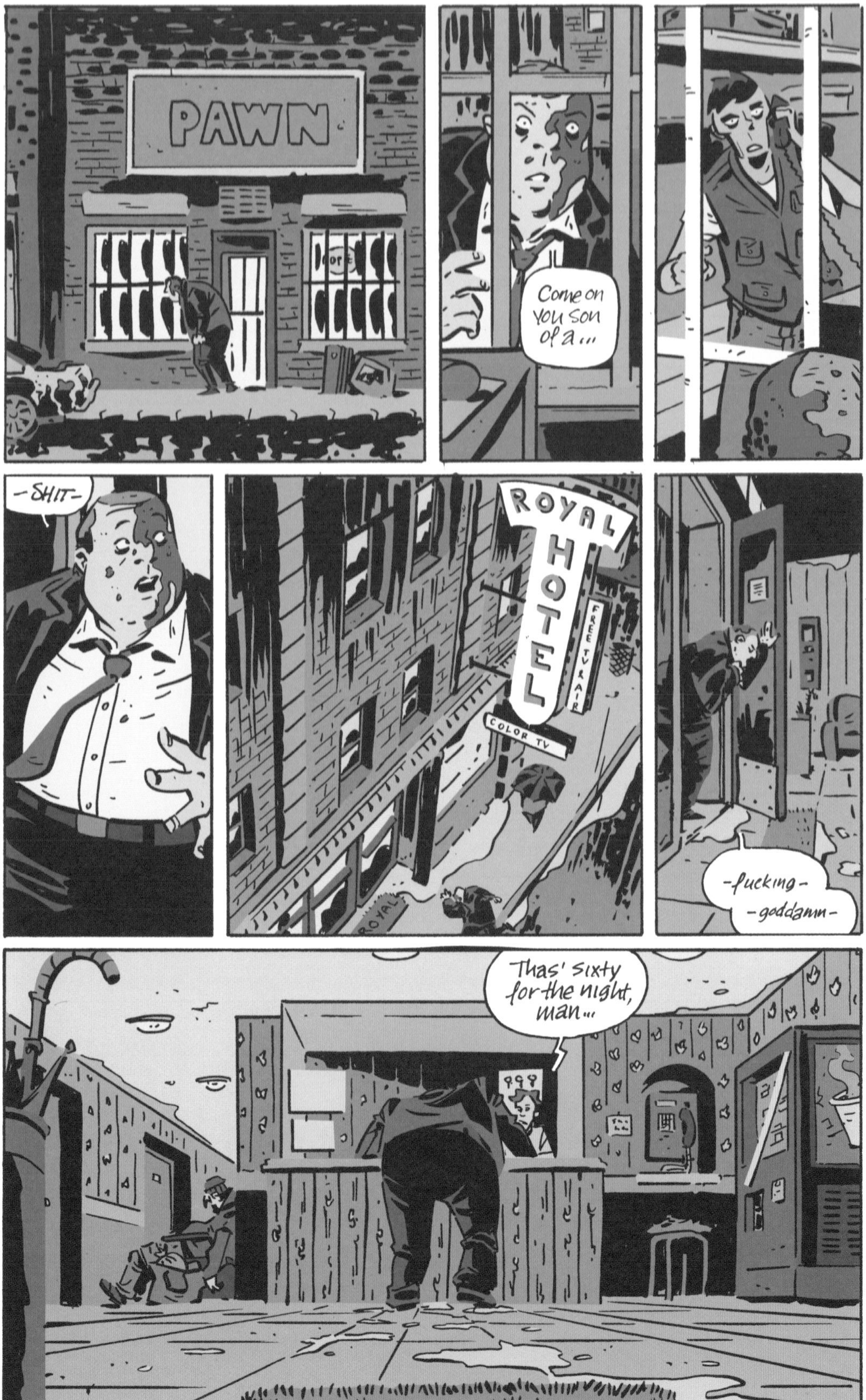
PAWN
Come on you son of a...
-SHIT-
ROYAL HOTEL
FREE TV & AIR
COLOR TV
ROYAL
-fucking-
-goddamn-
Thas' sixty for the night, man...

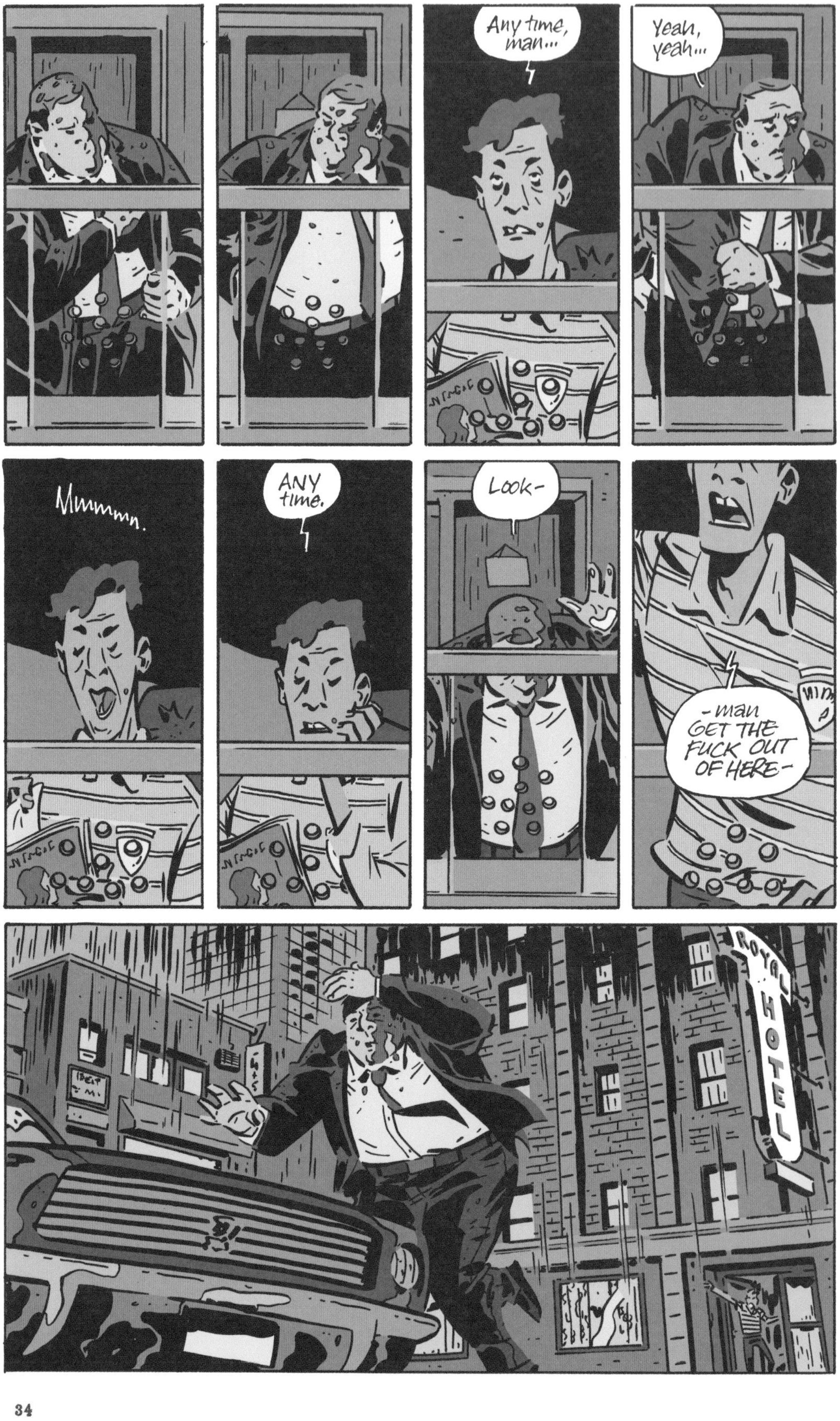

Any time, man...
Yeah, yeah...
Mmmmm.
ANY time.
Look-
-man GET THE FUCK OUT OF HERE-
ROYAL HOTEL

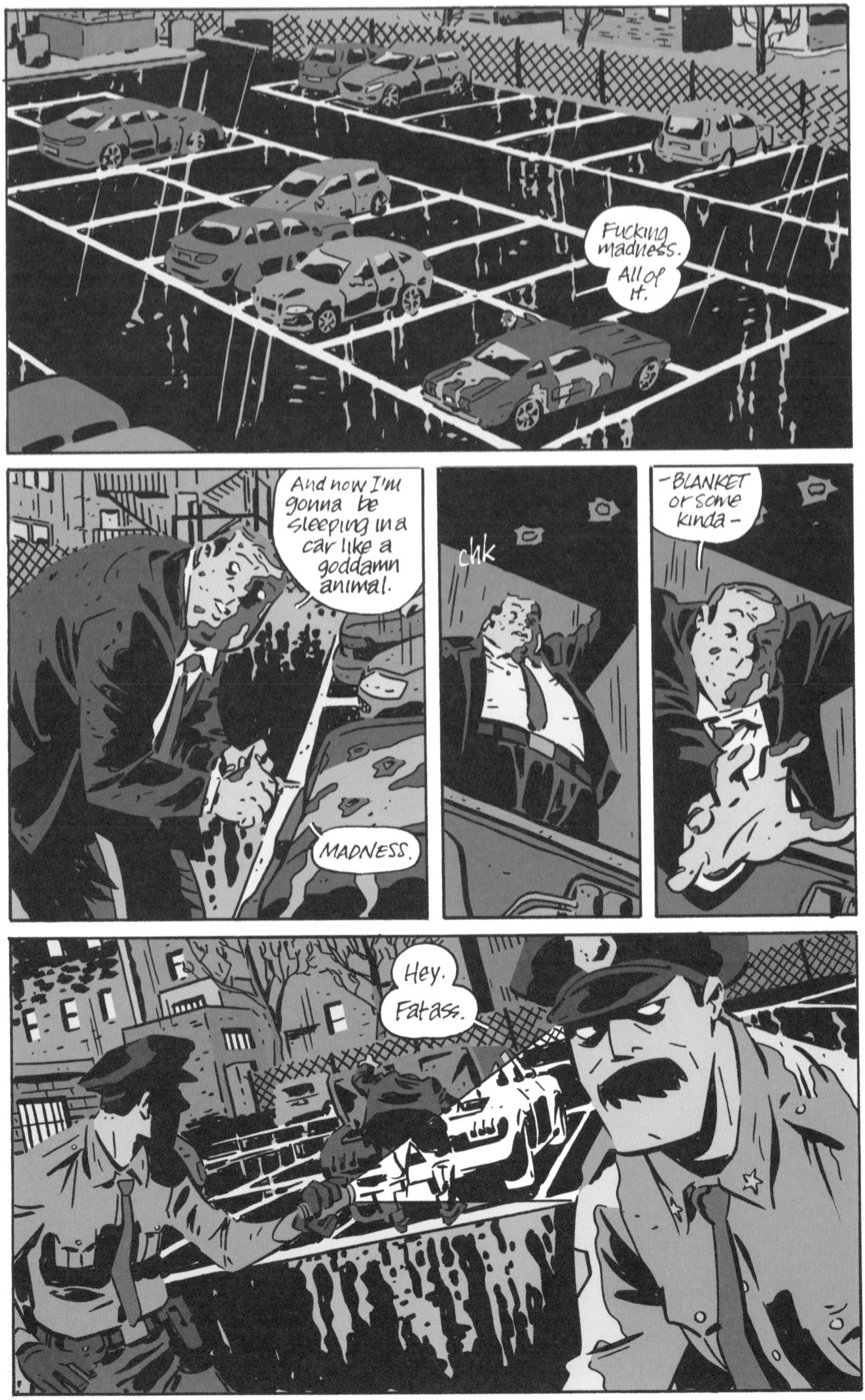
Fucking madness. All of it.
And now I'm gonna be sleeping in a car like a goddamn animal.
MADNESS.
chk
-BLANKET or some kinda-
Hey.
Fatass.

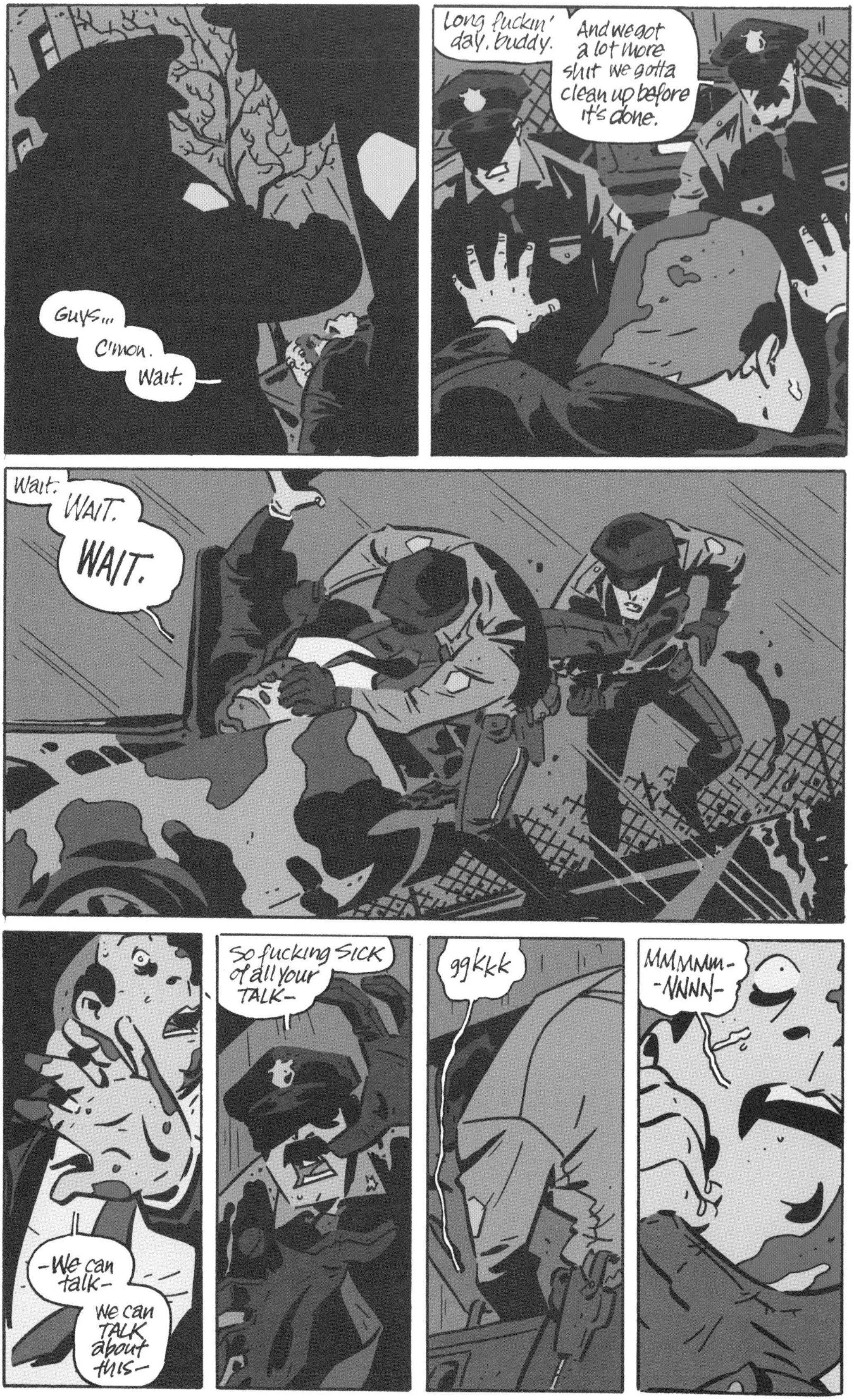
Guys...
C'mon.
Wait.
Long fuckin' day, buddy.
And we got a lot more shit we gotta clean up before it's done.
Wait.
WAIT.
WAIT.
-We can talk-
We can TALK about this-
So fucking SICK of all your TALK-
ggkkk
MMMMM-
-NNNN-

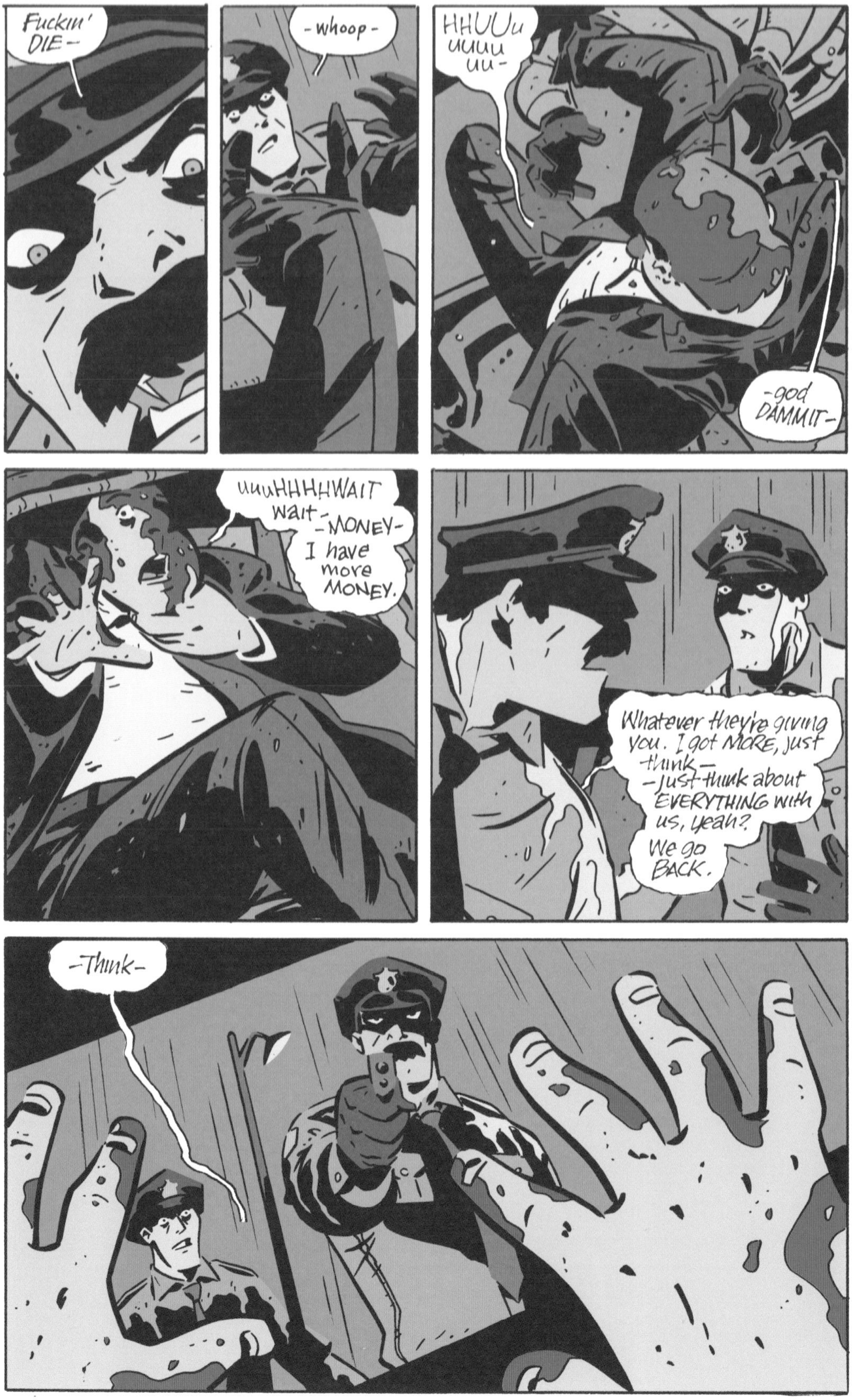
Fuckin' DIE—
-whoop-
HHUUu uuuu uu-
-god DAMMIT-
uuuHHHHWAIT wait- -MONEY- I have more MONEY.
Whatever they're giving you. I got MORE, just think— —just think about EVERYTHING with us, yeah? We go BACK.
-Think-

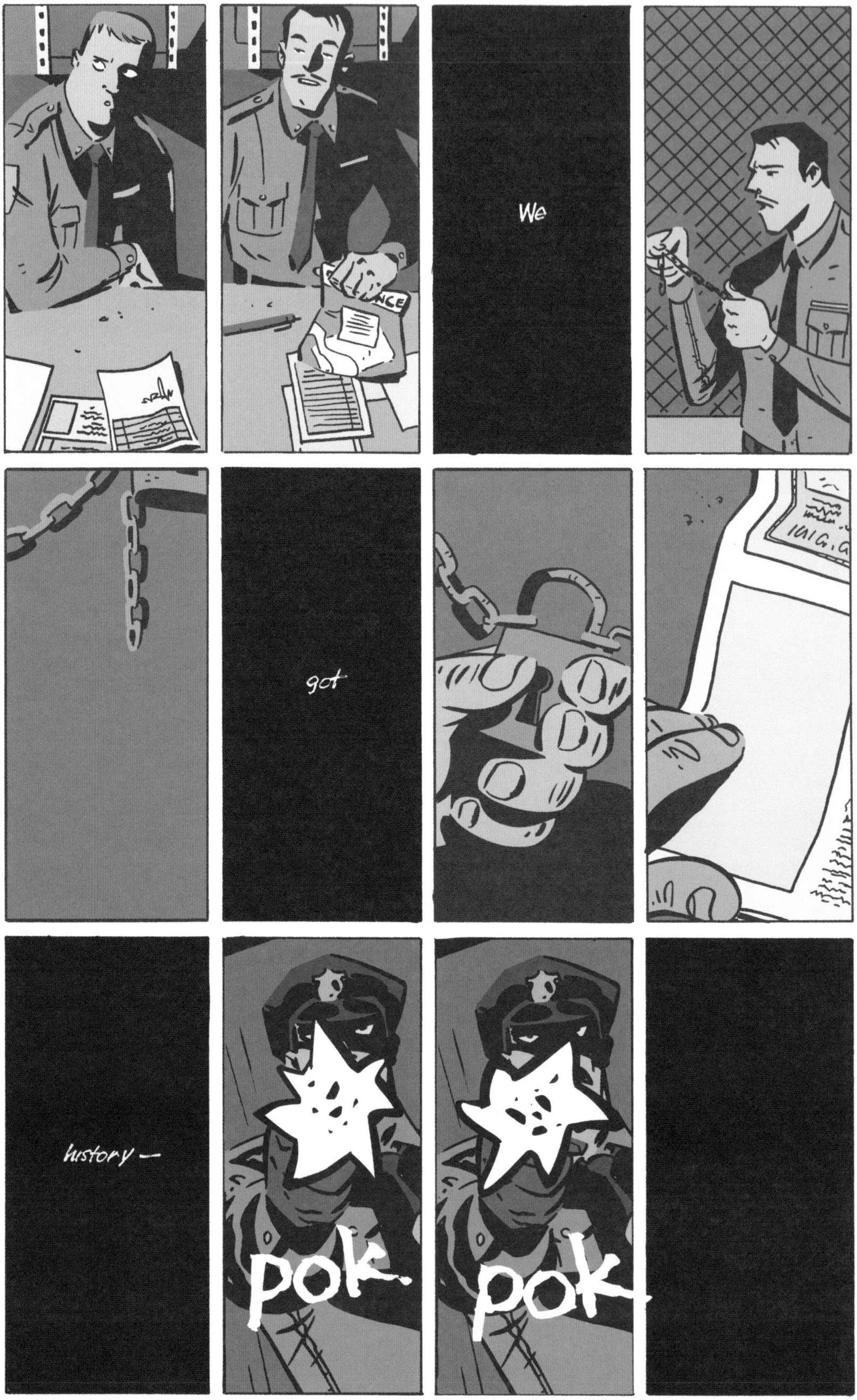
We
got
history —
pok
pok

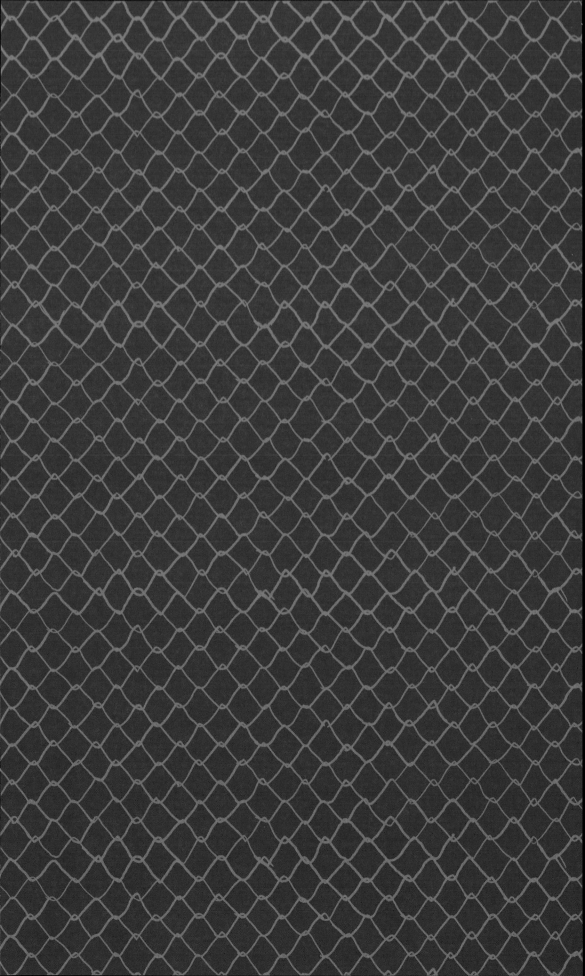

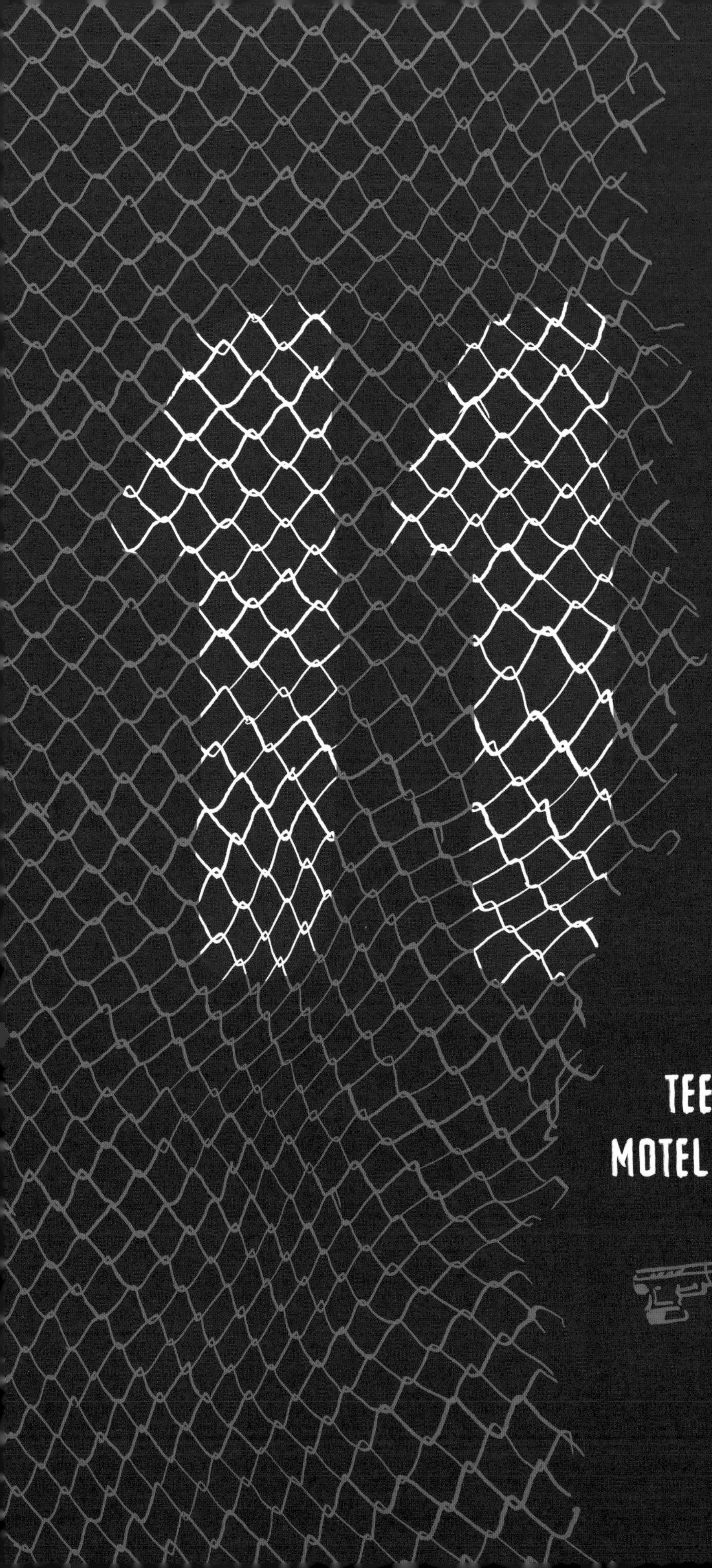

TEENAGE LEZBO MOTEL MAIDS ON SPEED

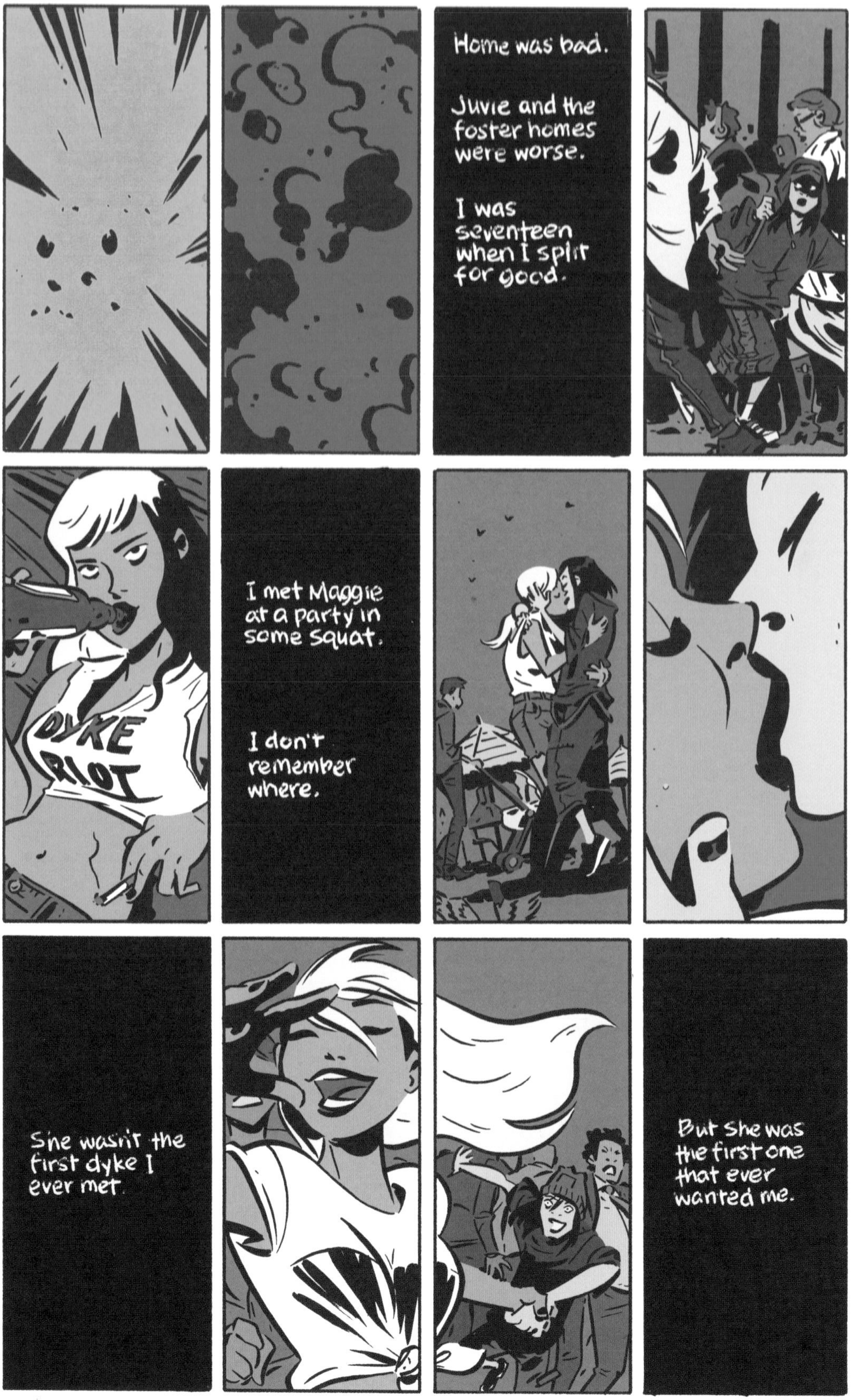
Home was bad.
Juvie and the foster homes were worse.
I was seventeen when I split for good.
I met Maggie at a party in some squat.
I don't remember where.
DYKE RIOT
She wasn't the first dyke I ever met.
But she was the first one that ever wanted me.

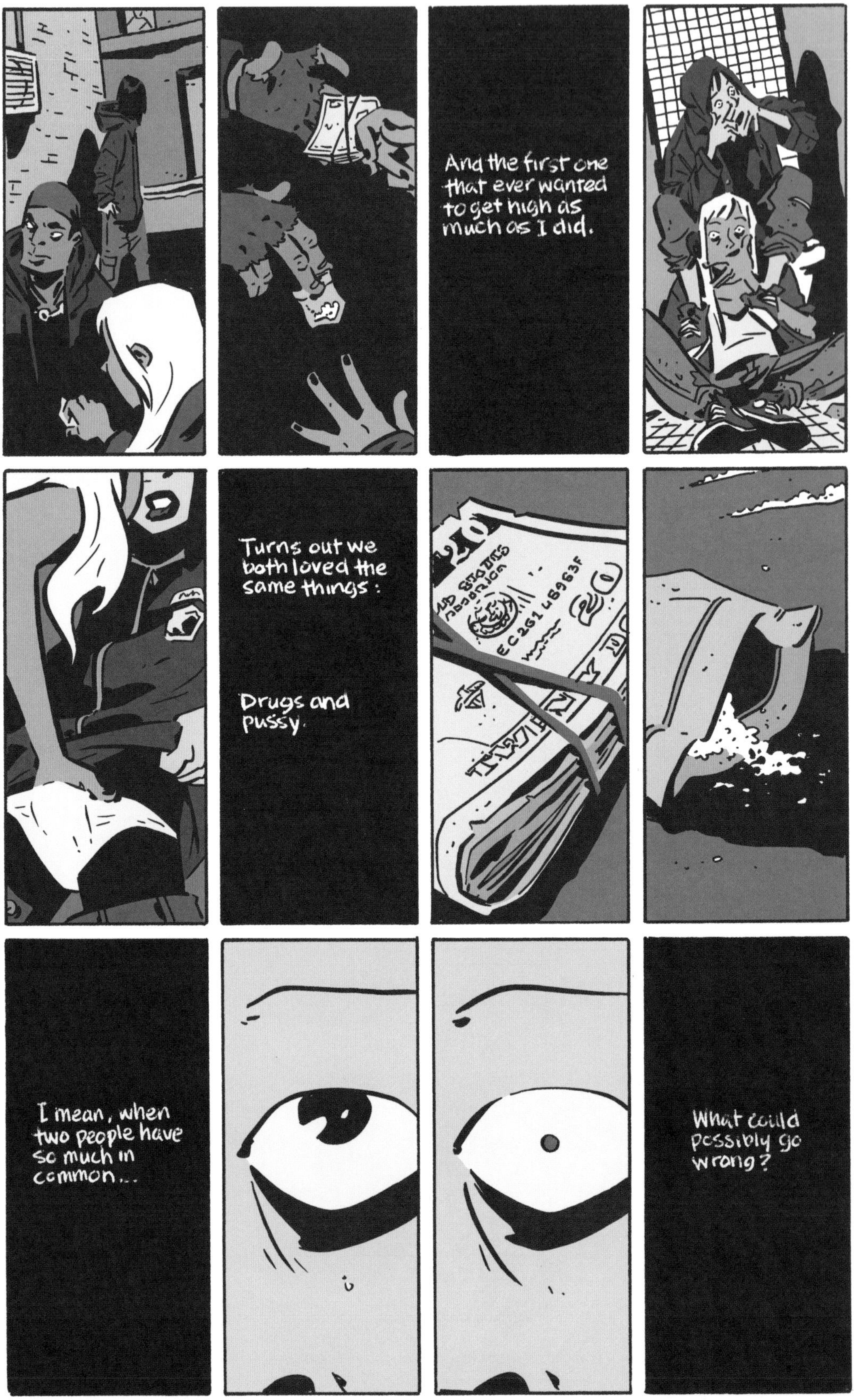
And the first one that ever wanted to get high as much as I did.
Turns out we both loved the same things:
Drugs and pussy.
I mean, when two people have so much in common...
What could possibly go wrong?

Well, turns out getting money to buy drugs kinda becomes a real thing after a point.

I'd steal for it.

Maggie'd sleep with dudes for it.

Well. "Sleep."

Sometimes I thought she enjoyed it.

I'd get jealous.

Baby, never trust a junkie, she'd say.

Still hurt.

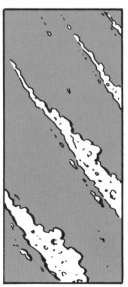

But y'know what's good for pain?

Drugs and pussy.

So it all worked out.

One day Maggie gets a lead on a job working as maids for a shitty little no-tell motel kinda-place.

Some guy knew some guy Maggie knew.

Harmless, she said.

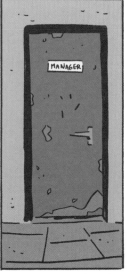

Don't fuck this up for us,

she whispered at me.

During our "interview."

That's when I realized why *Harmless* here always wore sweatpants.

So you wouldn't hear his zipper.

Anyway we got the gig.

From that point on, it was party time.

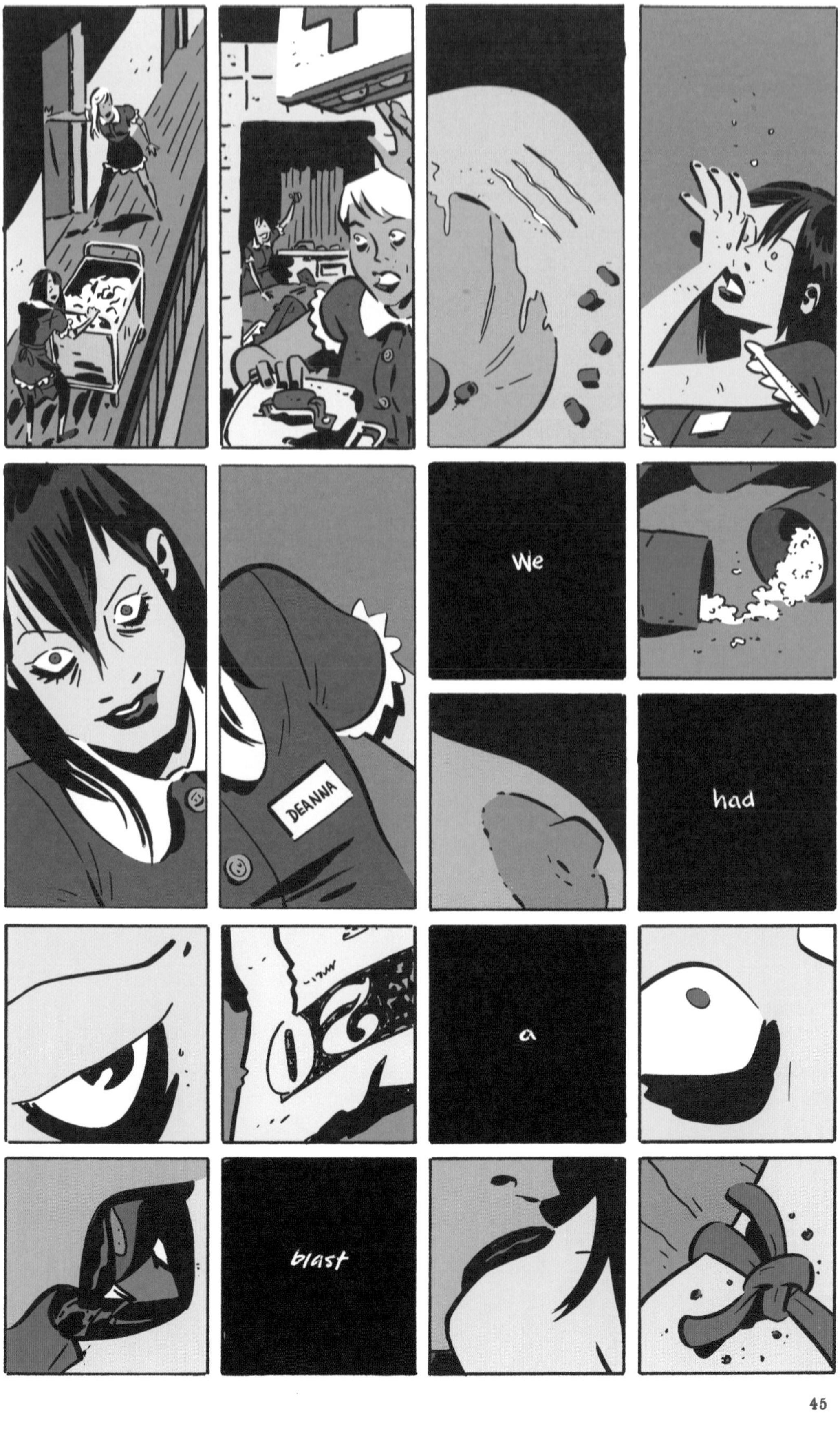
DEANNA
We
had
a
blast

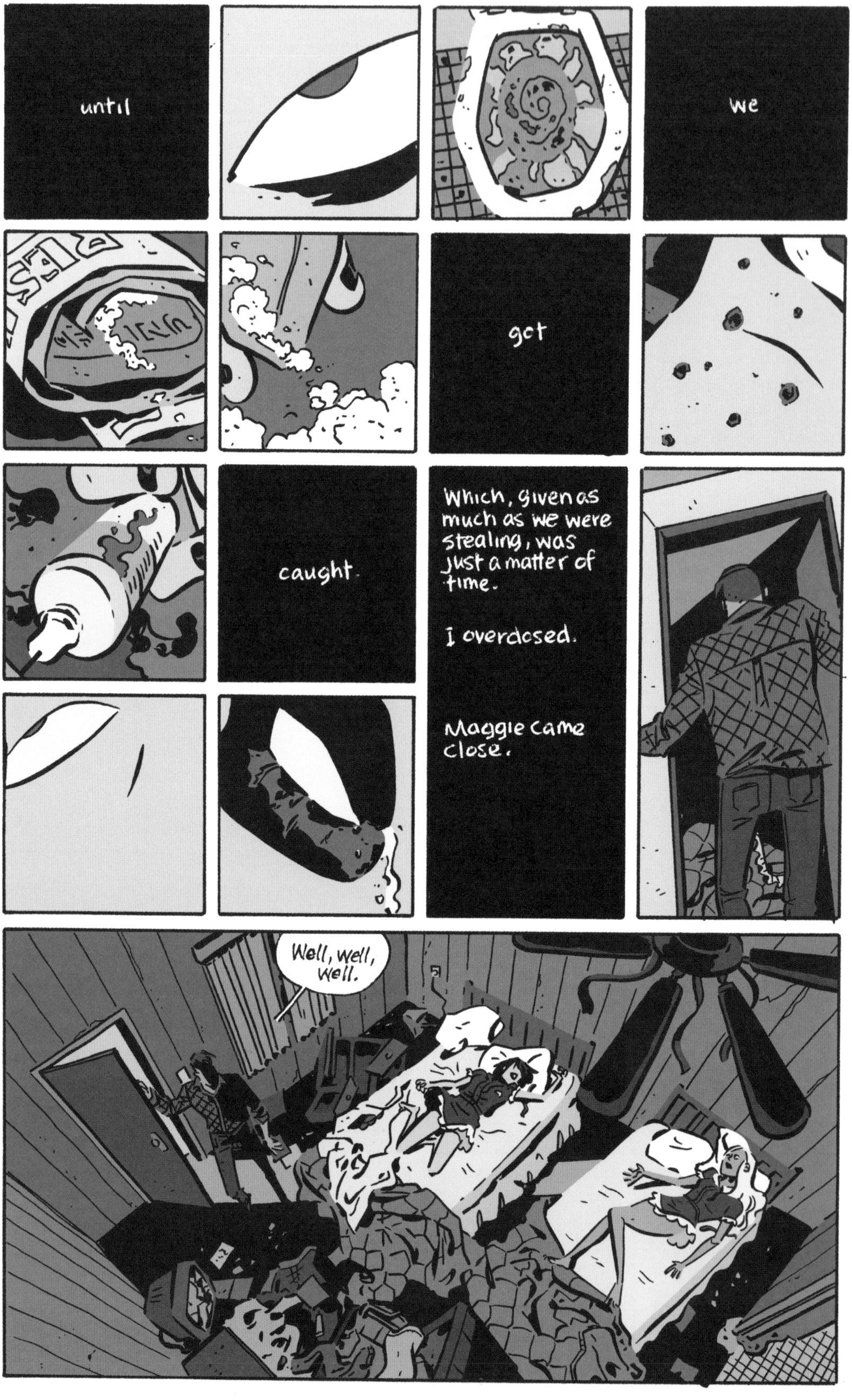

until
we
get
caught.
Which, given as much as we were stealing, was just a matter of time.
I overdosed.
Maggie came close.
Well, well, well.

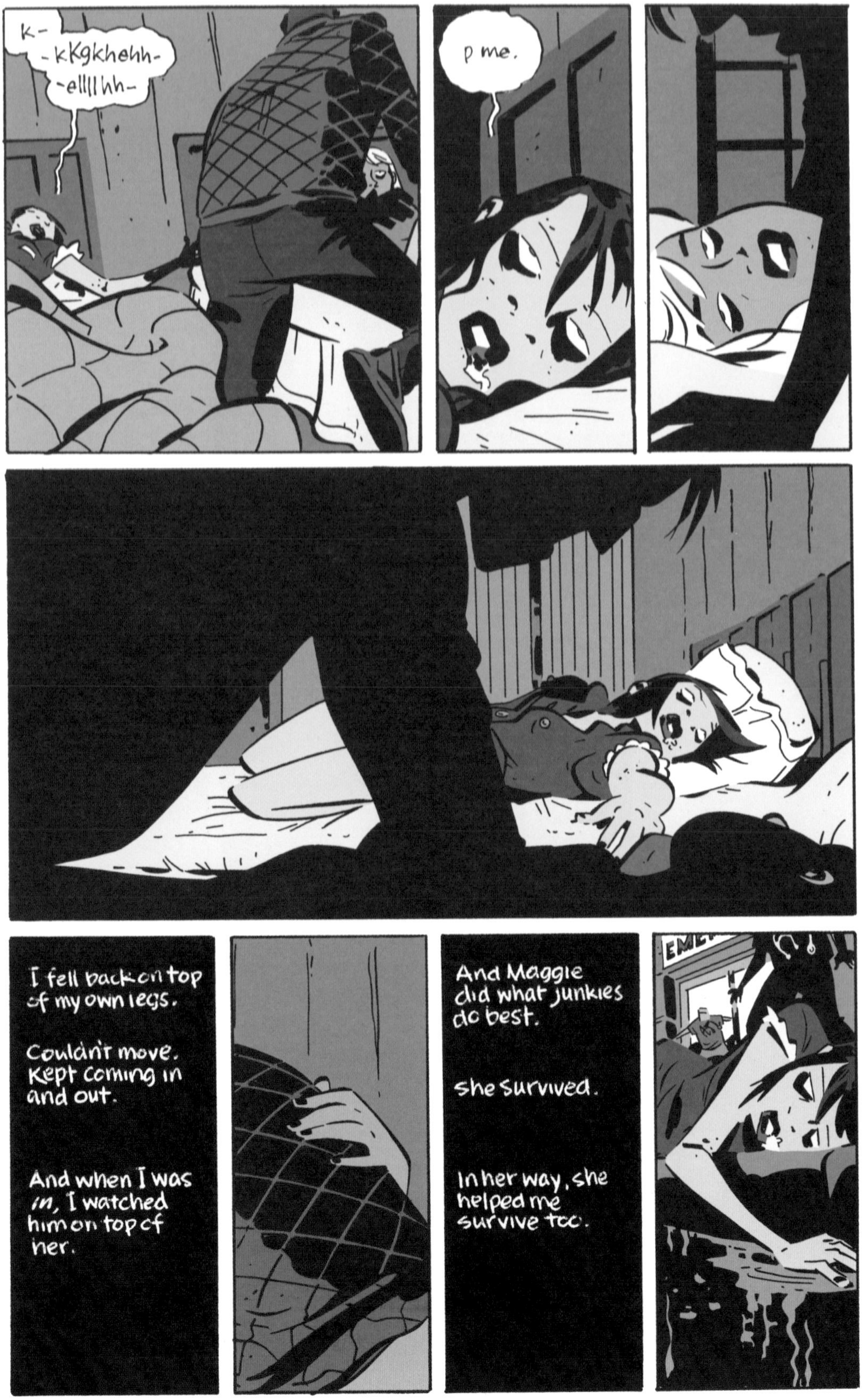

K-
-KKgkhehh-
-ellllhh-
p me.
I fell back on top of my own legs.
Couldn't move. Kept coming in and out.
And when I was in, I watched him on top of her.
And Maggie did what junkies do best.
She survived.
In her way, she helped me survive too.

They kicked me out with a crutch, some penicillin for the staph infection in my hip, and two legs that didn't work so great anymore.

They still send the bills.

I still ignore them.

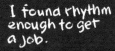

I found a rhythm enough to get a job.

I stayed employable enough to pay for my medication.

And so on and so forth.

Until *he* showed up in my life, with a new rhythm and the promise of a life filled with fabulous amounts of unending cash.

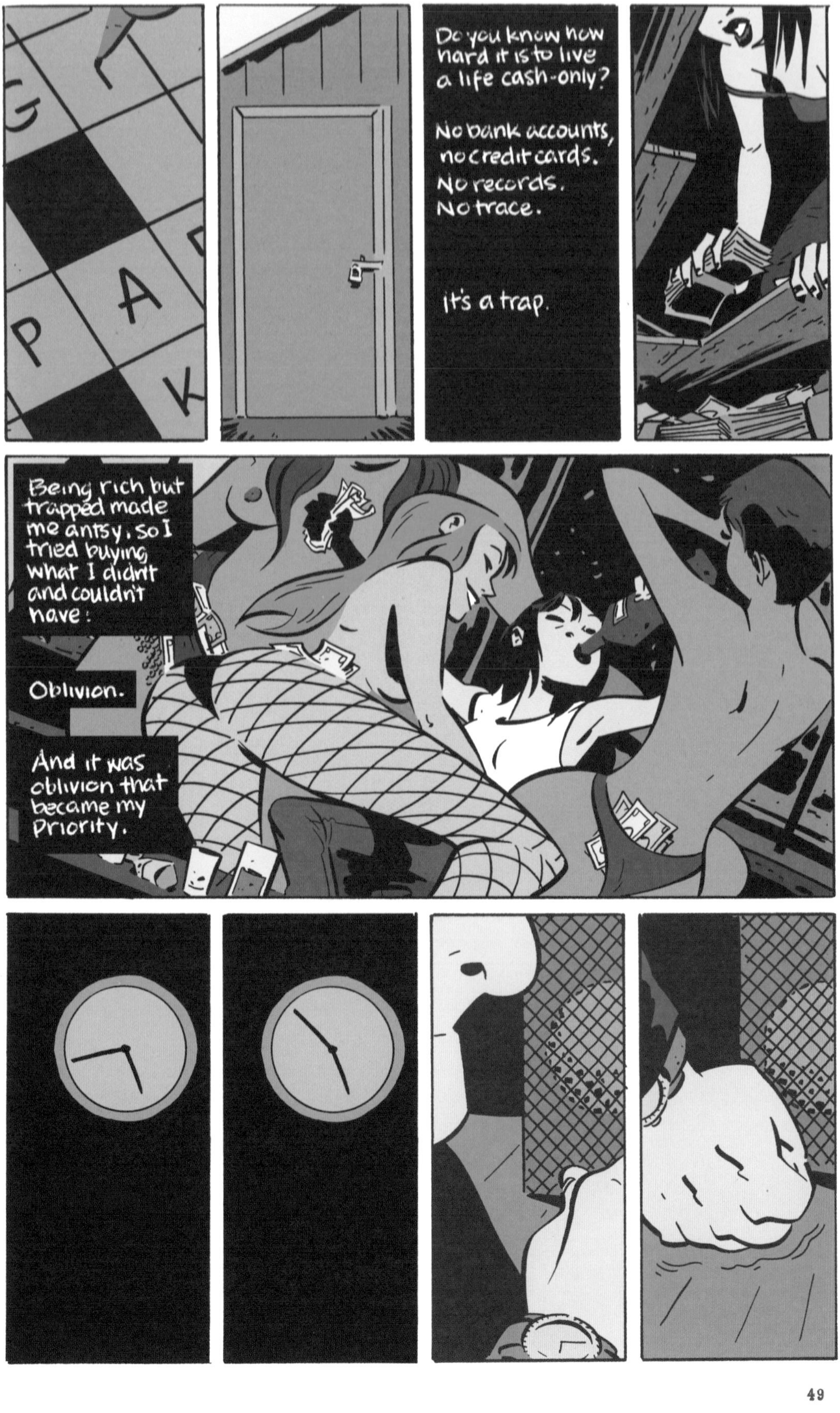

G
P A
P
K
Do you know how hard it is to live a life cash-only?
No bank accounts, no credit cards.
No records.
No trace.
it's a trap.
Being rich but trapped made me antsy, so I tried buying what I didn't and couldn't have:
Oblivion.
And it was oblivion that became my Priority.

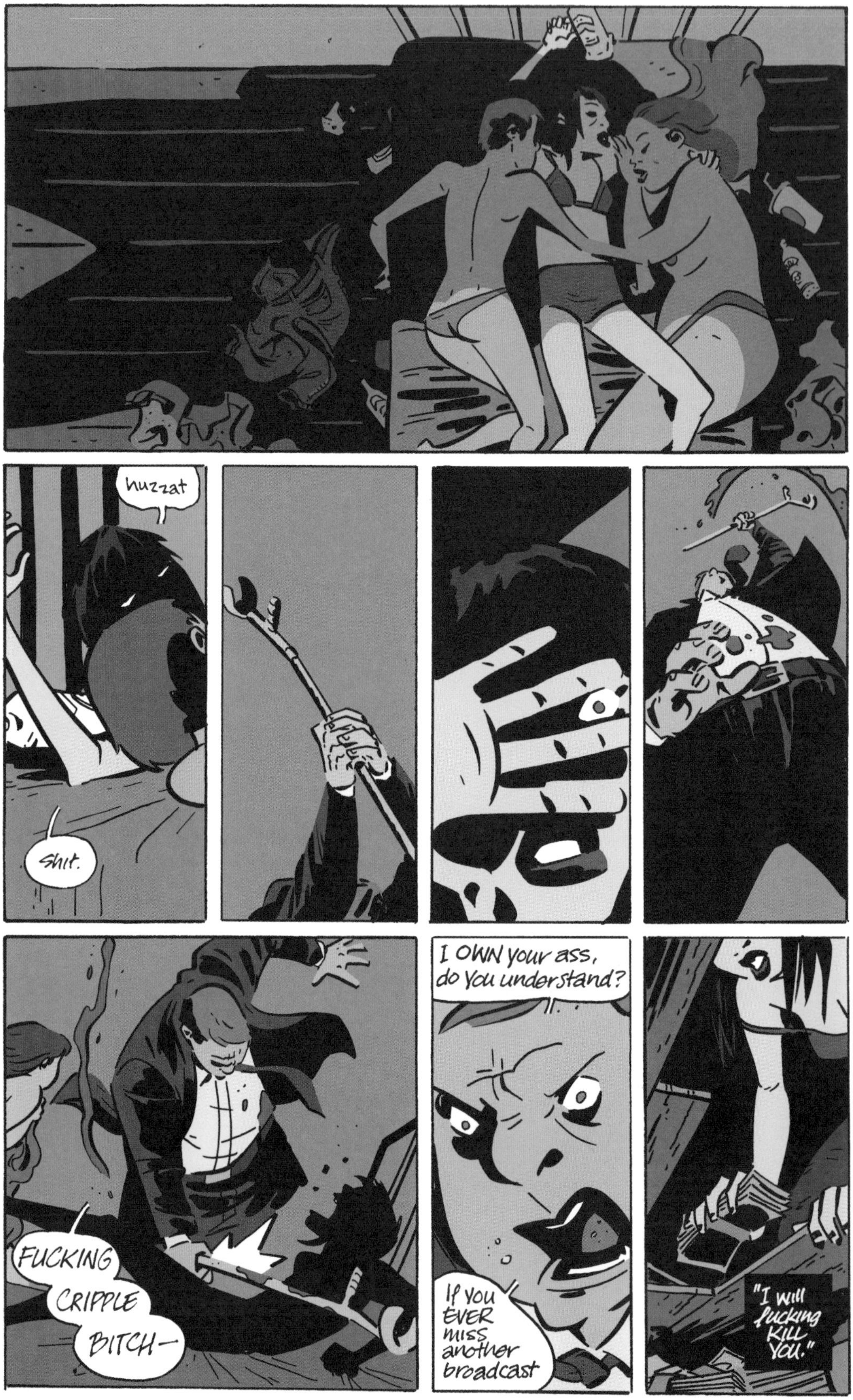
huzzat
shit.
FUCKING CRIPPLE BITCH—
I OWN your ass, do you understand?
If you EVER miss another broadcast
"I will fucking KILL YOU."

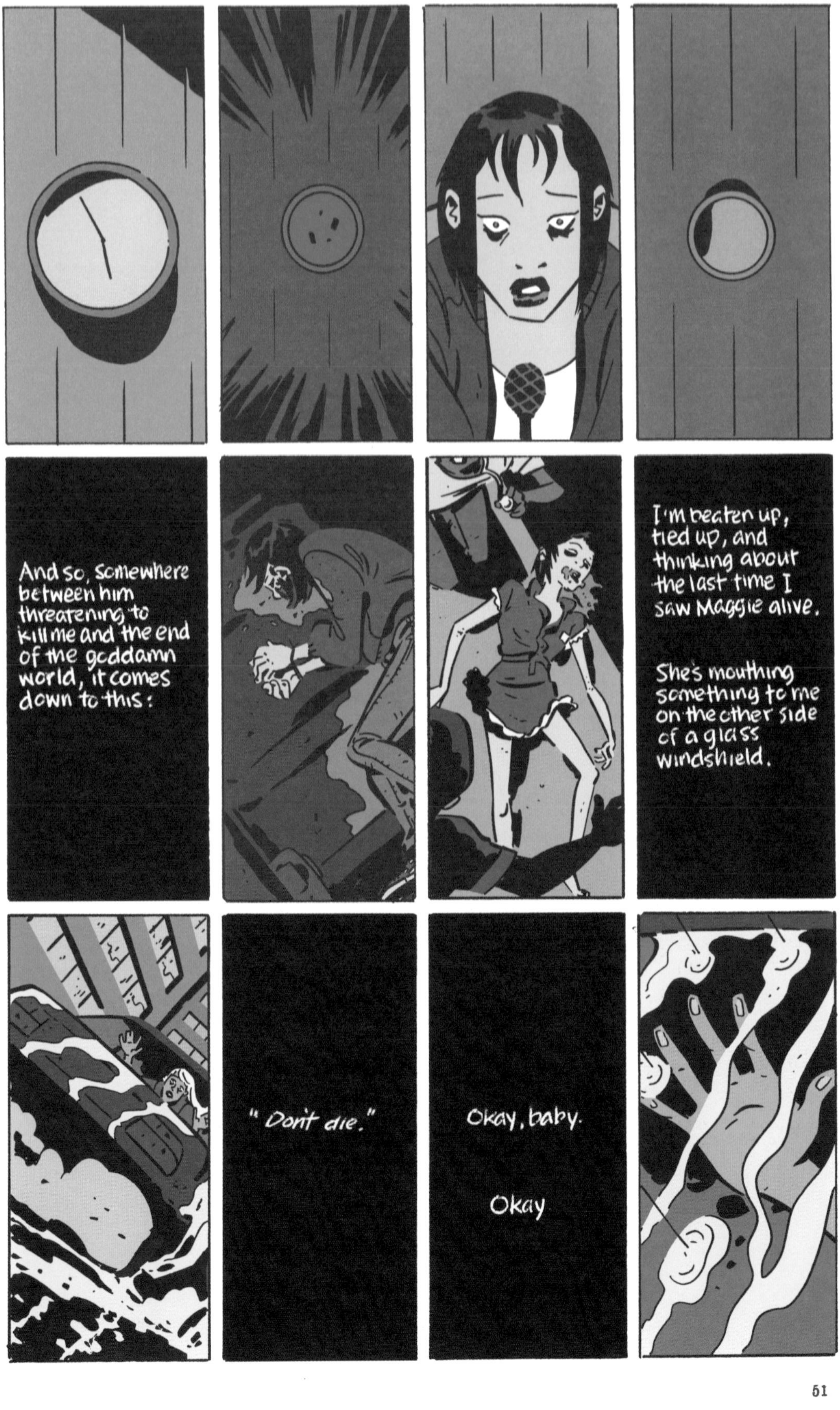
And so, somewhere between him threatening to kill me and the end of the goddamn world, it comes down to this:
I'm beaten up, tied up, and thinking about the last time I saw Maggie alive.
She's mouthing something to me on the other side of a glass windshield.
"Don't die."
Okay, baby.
Okay.

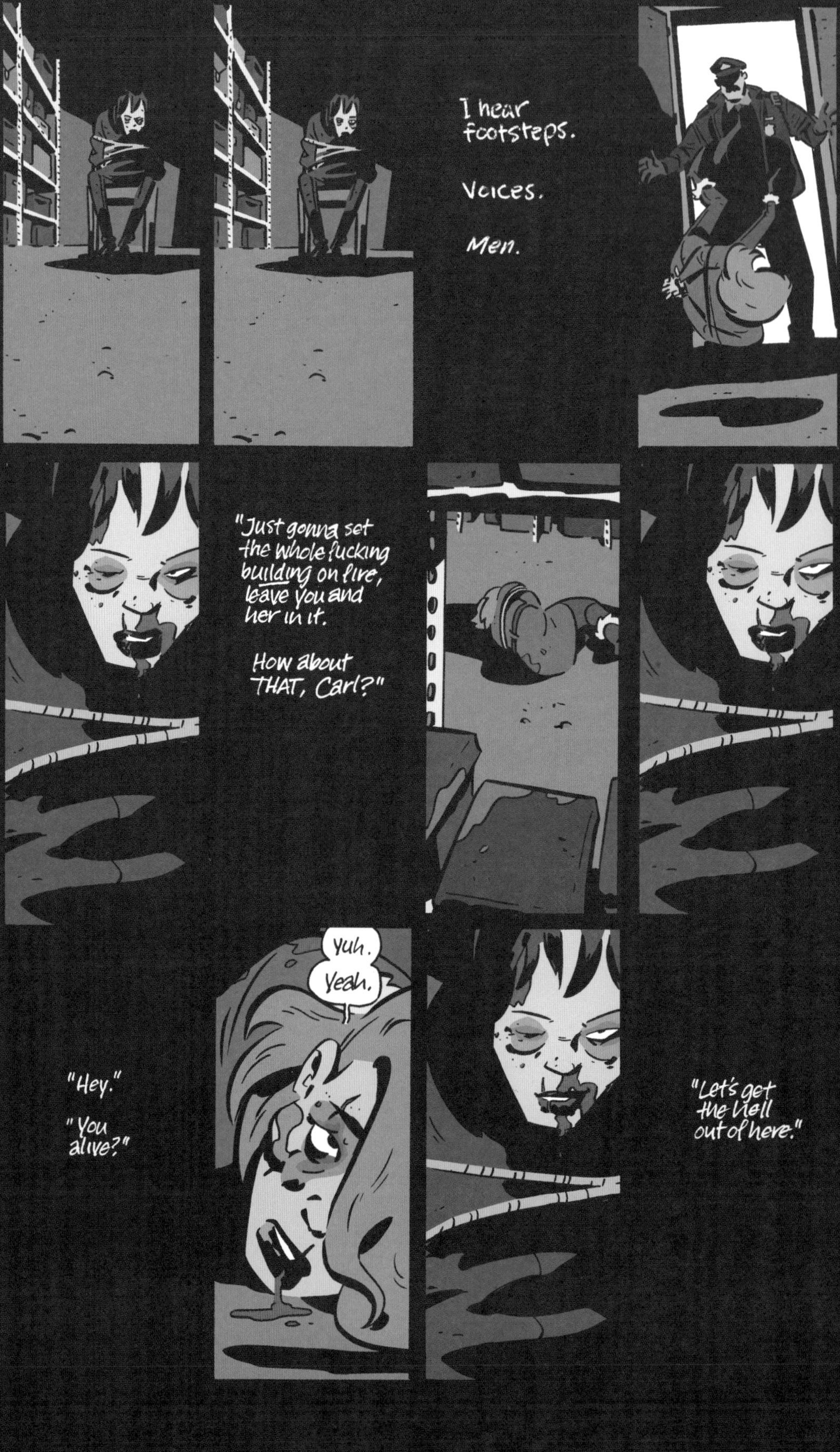
I hear footsteps.
Voices.
Men.
"Just gonna set the whole fucking building on fire, leave you and her in it.
How about THAT, Carl?"
"Hey."
"You alive?"
Yuh.
Yeah.
"Let's get the hell out of here."

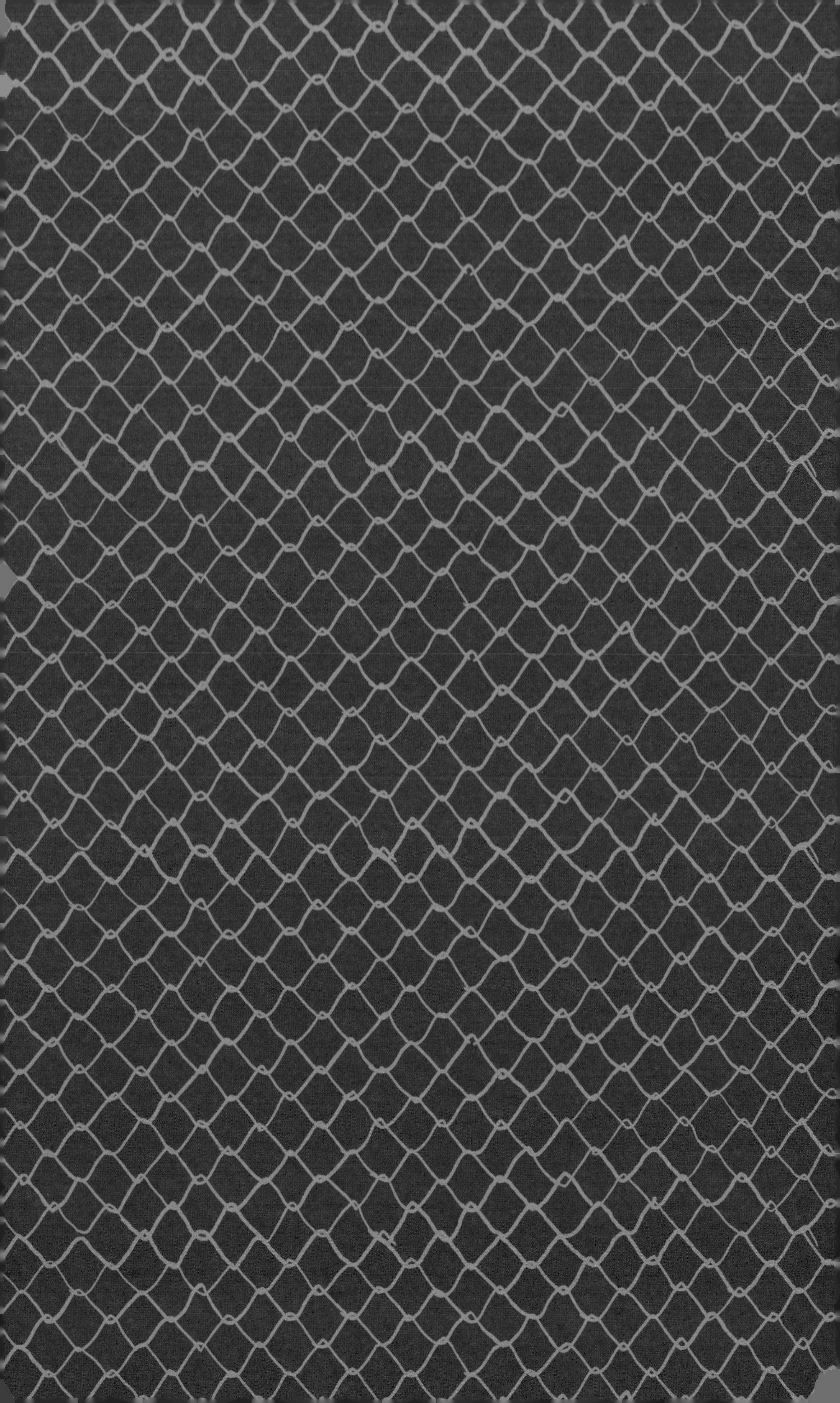

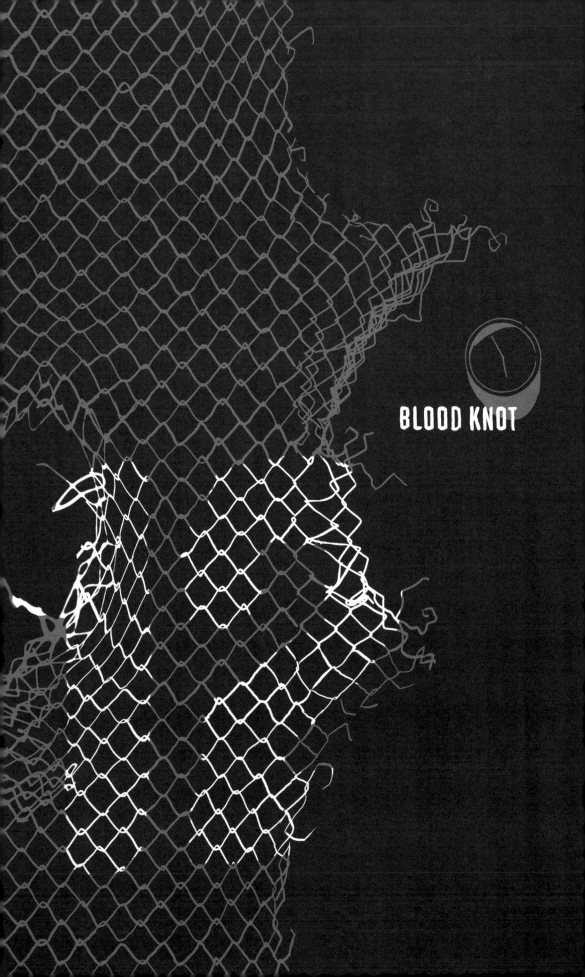

BLOOD KNOT

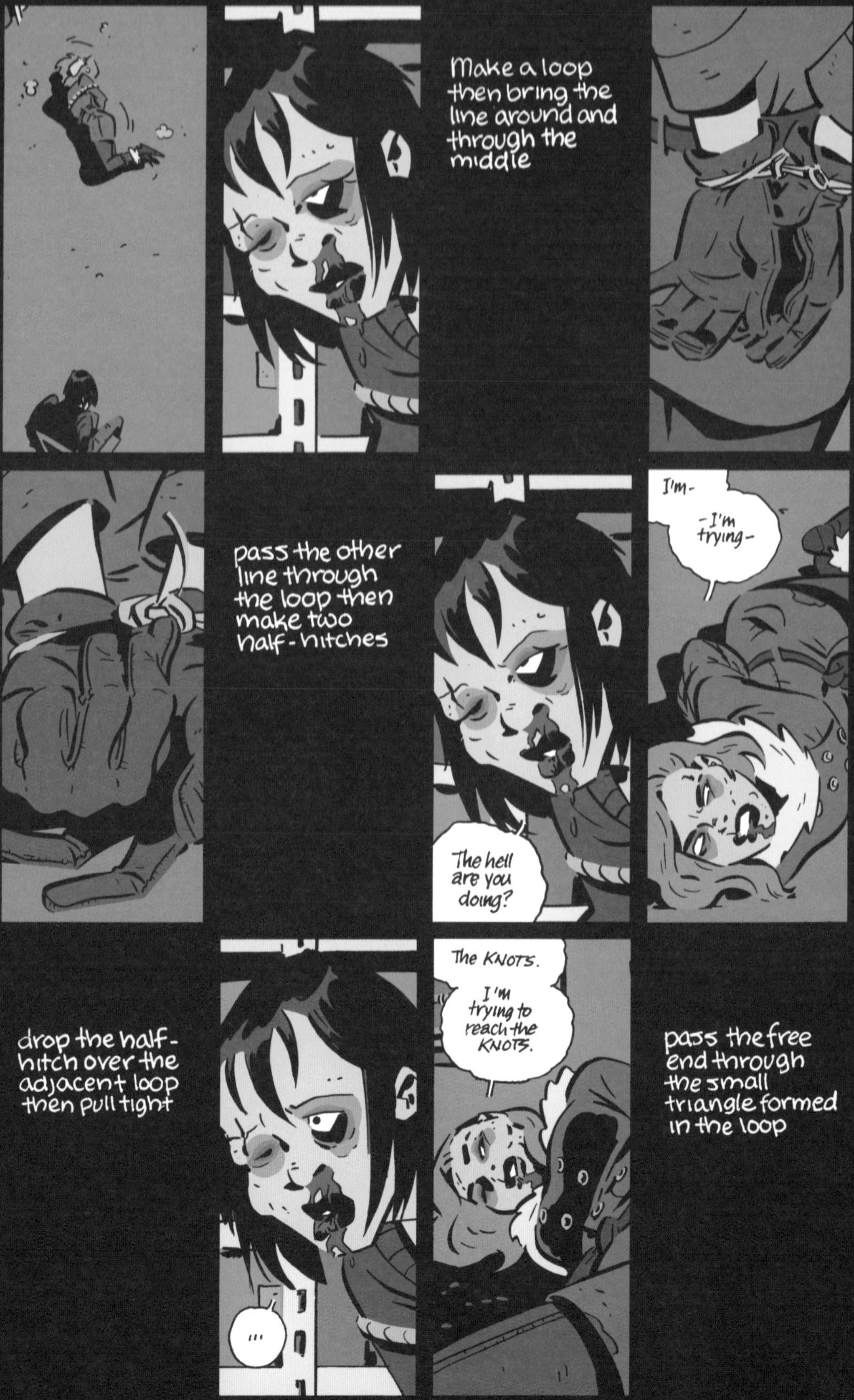
Make a loop then bring the line around and through the middle
pass the other line through the loop then make two half-hitches
The hell are you doing?
I'm-
-I'm trying-
drop the half-hitch over the adjacent loop then pull tight
...
The KNOTS.
I'm trying to reach the KNOTS.
pass the free end through the small triangle formed in the loop

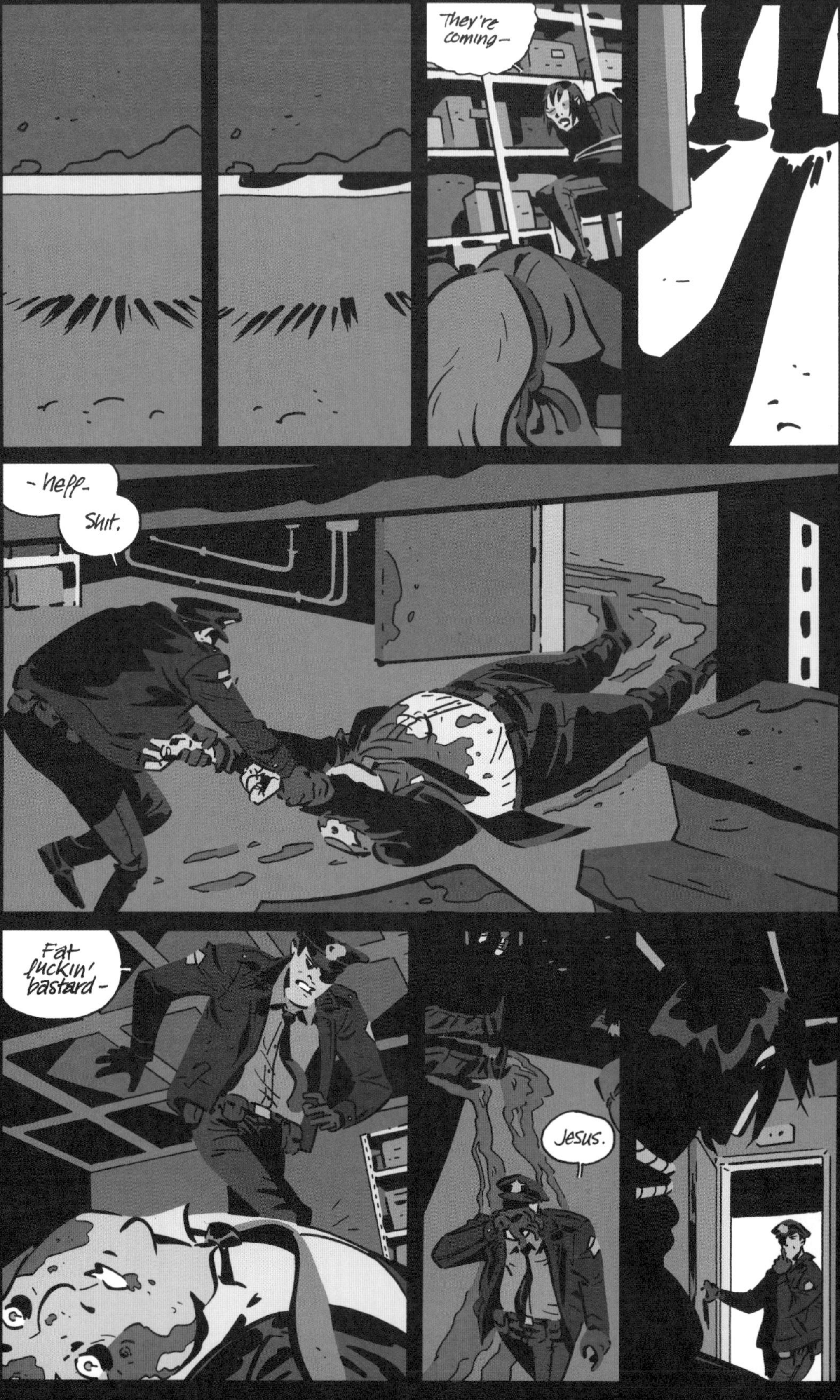
They're coming-
-hepp-
Shit.
Fat fuckin' bastard-
Jesus.

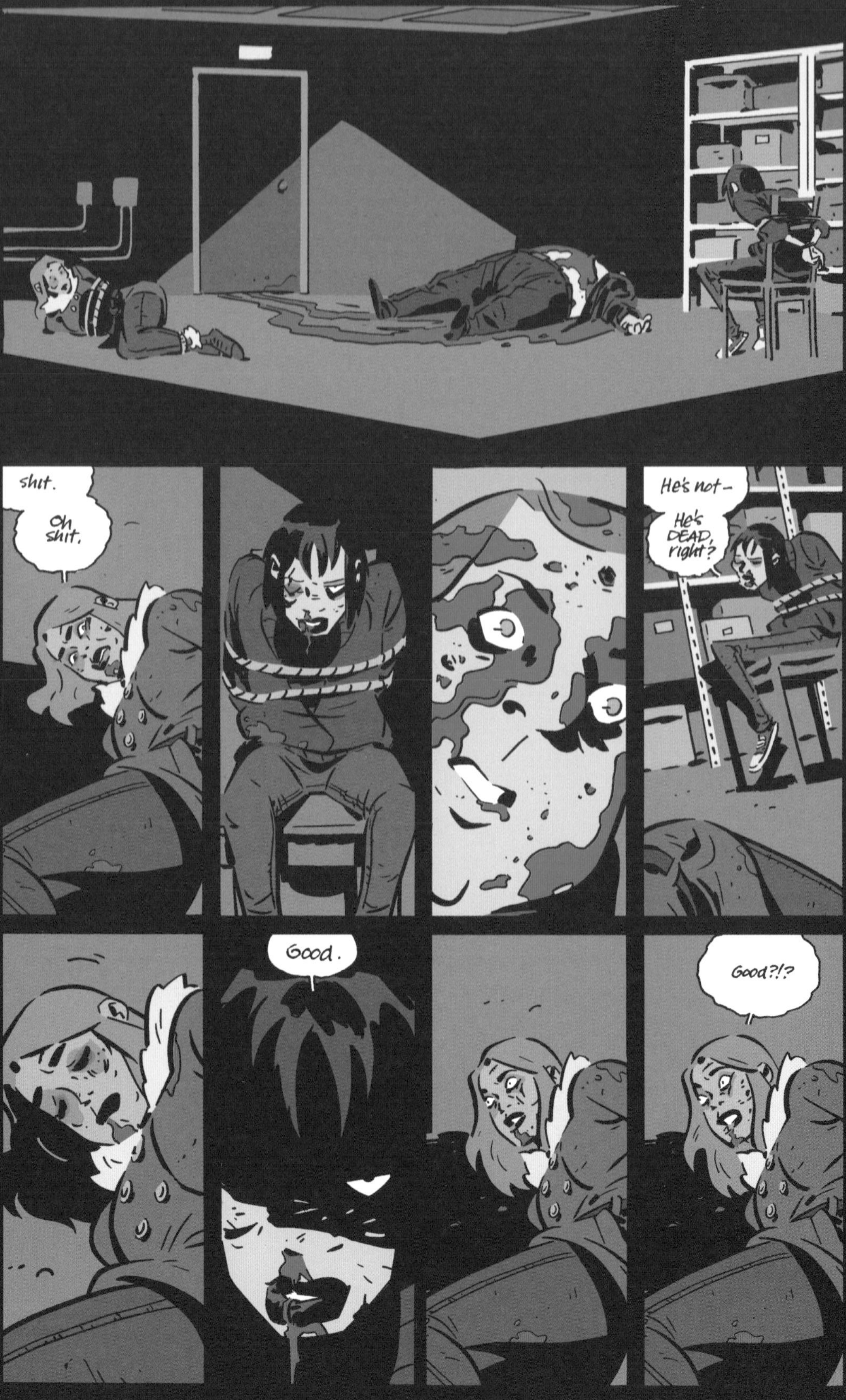
shit.
Oh shit.
He's not-
He's DEAD, right?
Good.
Good?!?

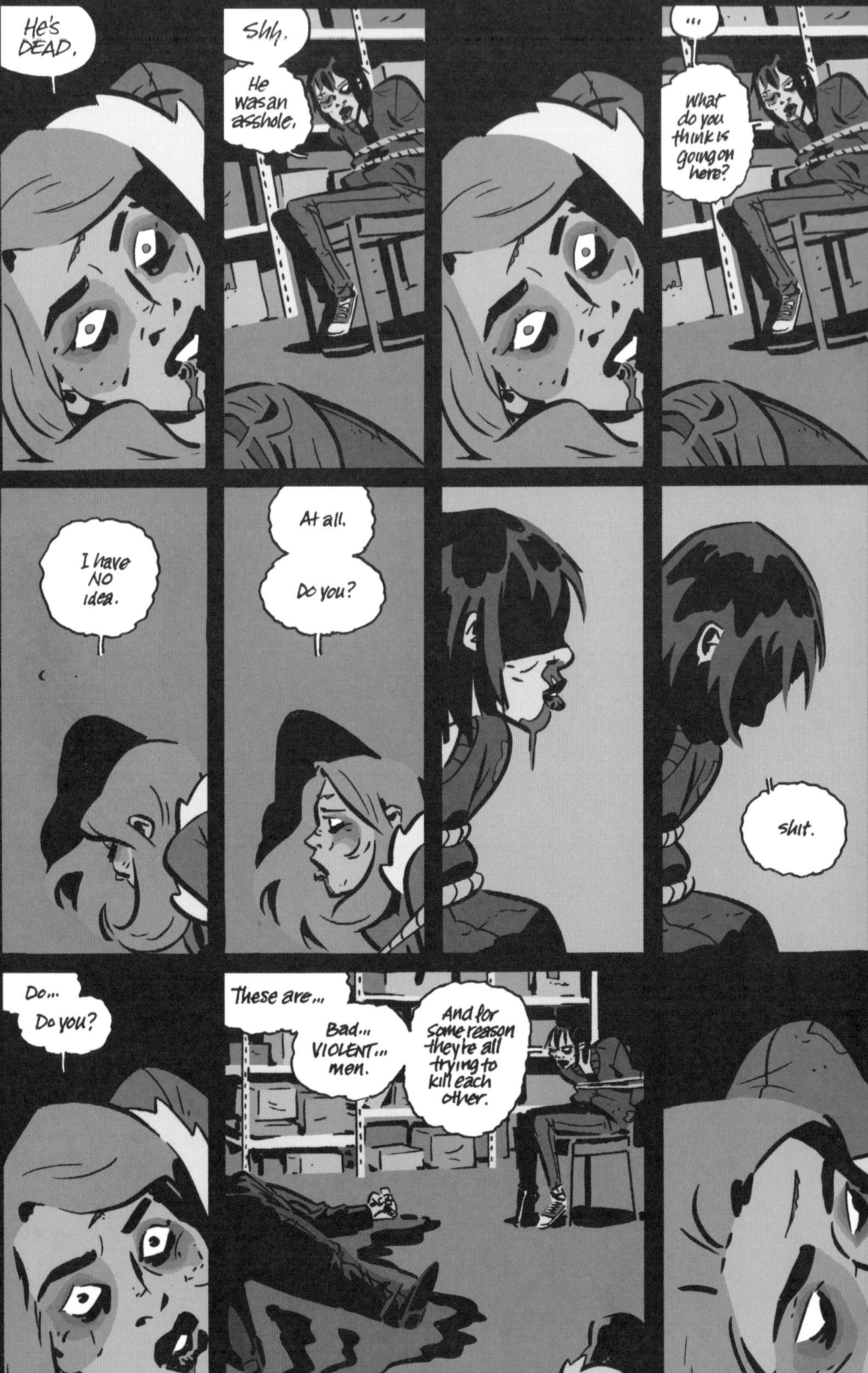

He's DEAD.
Shh.
He was an asshole.
...
What do you think is going on here?
I have NO idea.
At all.
Do you?
shit.
Do... Do you?
These are...
Bad... VIOLENT... men.
And for some reason they're all trying to kill each other.

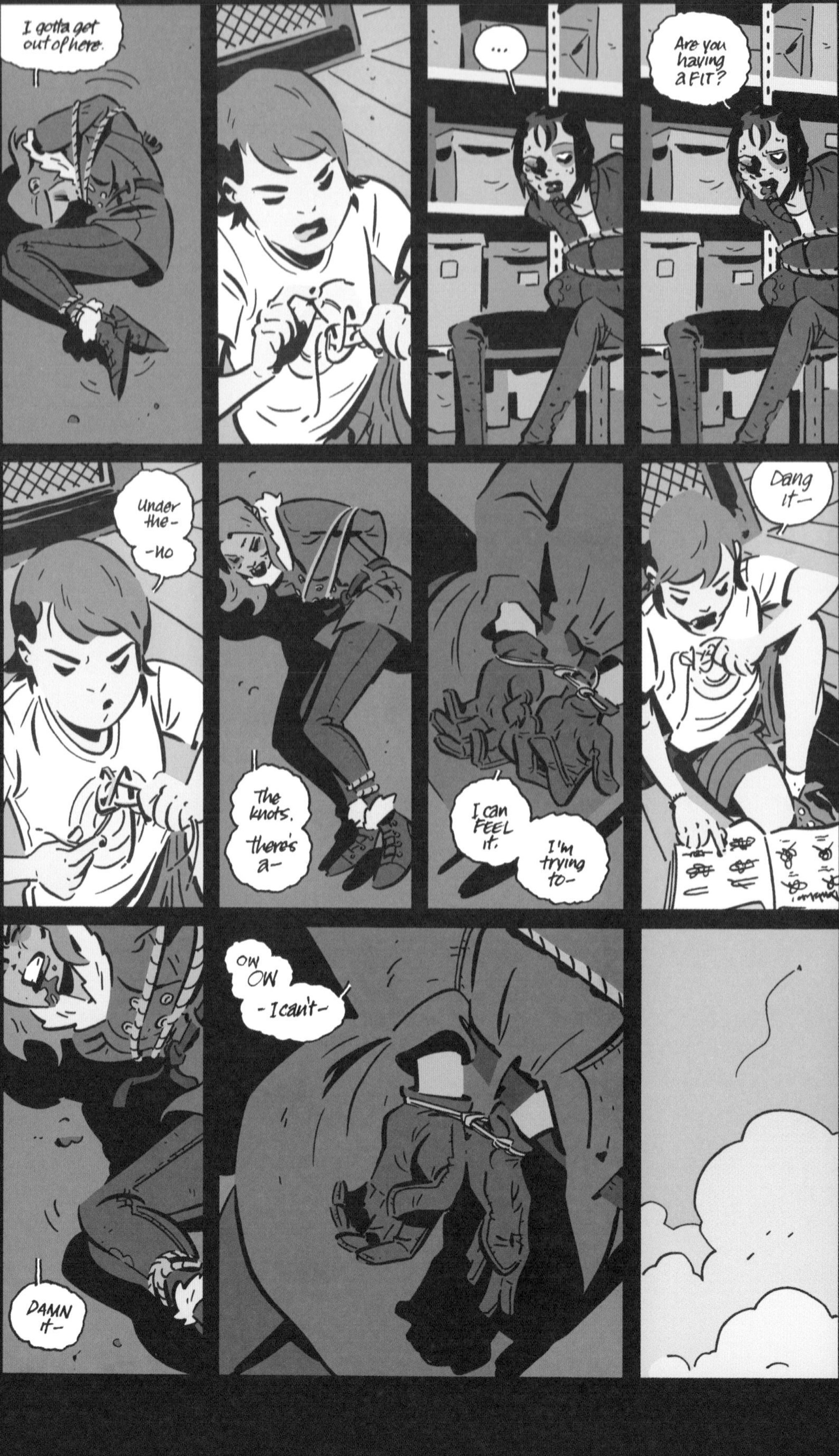

I gotta get out of here.
...
Are you having a FIT?
Under the-
-no
The knots.
there's a-
I can FEEL it.
I'm trying to-
Dang it-
DAMN it-
OW OW
-I can't-

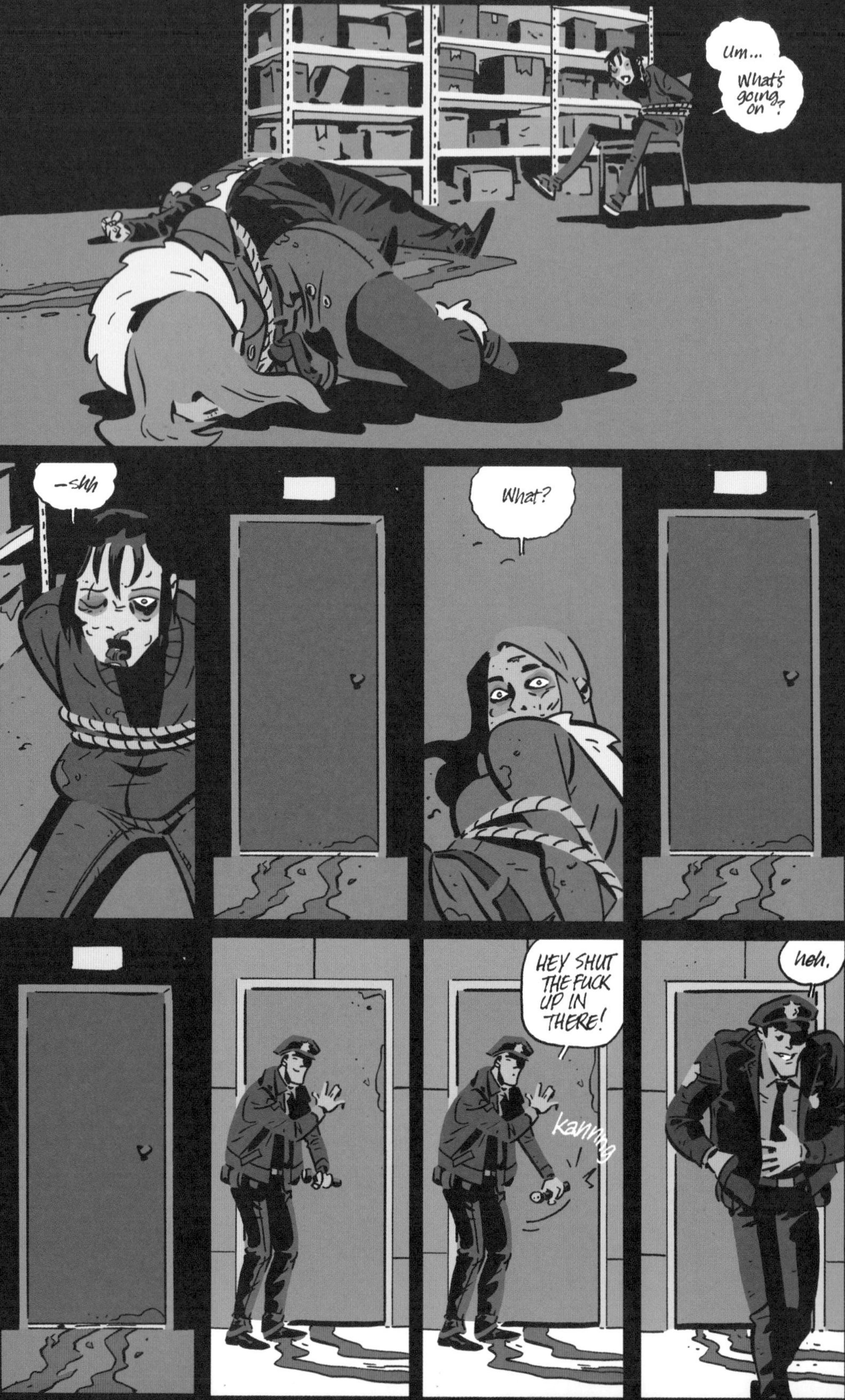
Um...
What's going on?
-shh
What?
HEY SHUT THE FUCK UP IN THERE!
kanng
heh.

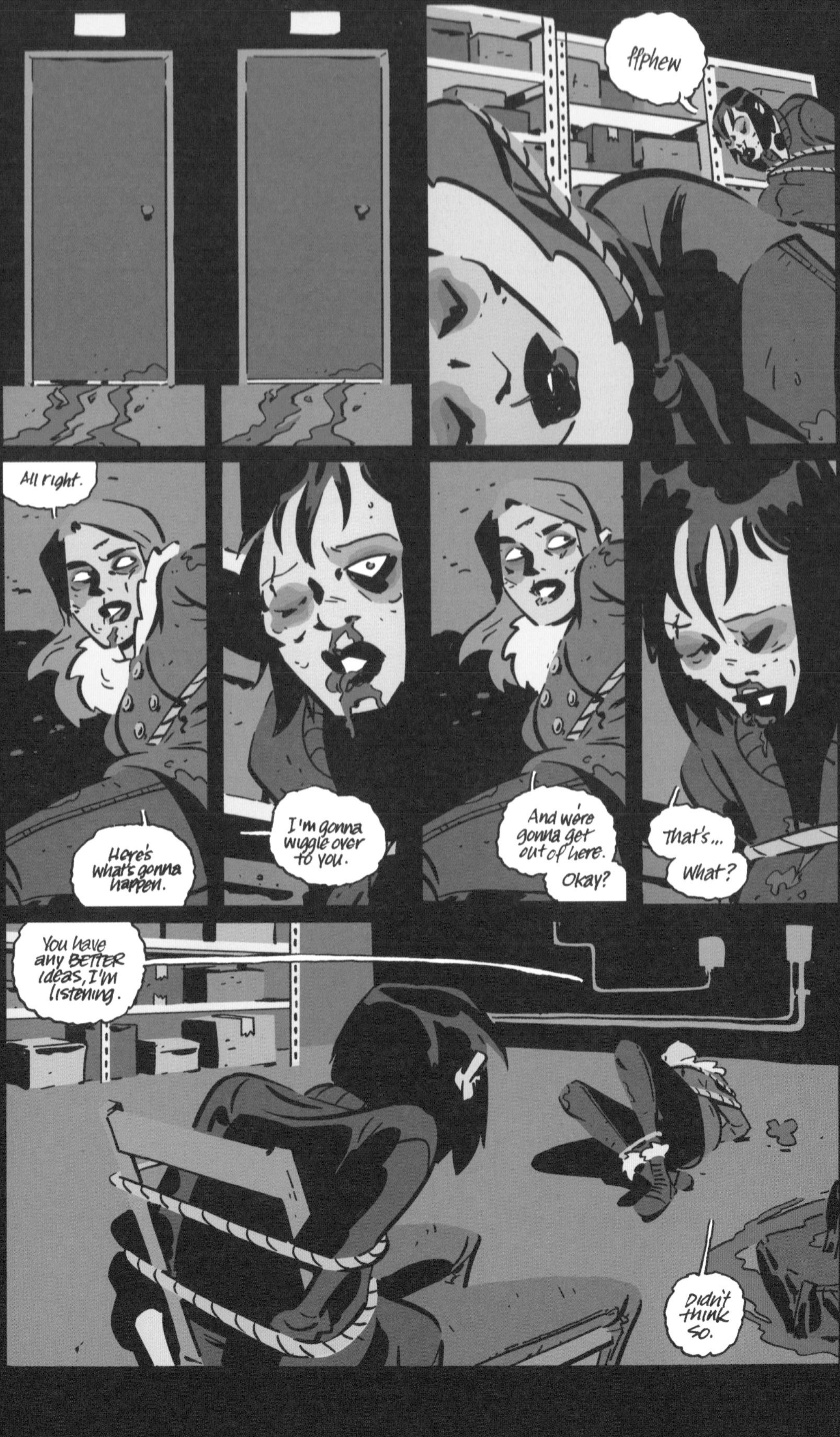
ffphew
All right.
Here's what's gonna happen.
I'm gonna wiggle over to you.
And we're gonna get out of here.
Okay?
That's...
What?
You have any BETTER ideas, I'm listening.
Didn't think so.

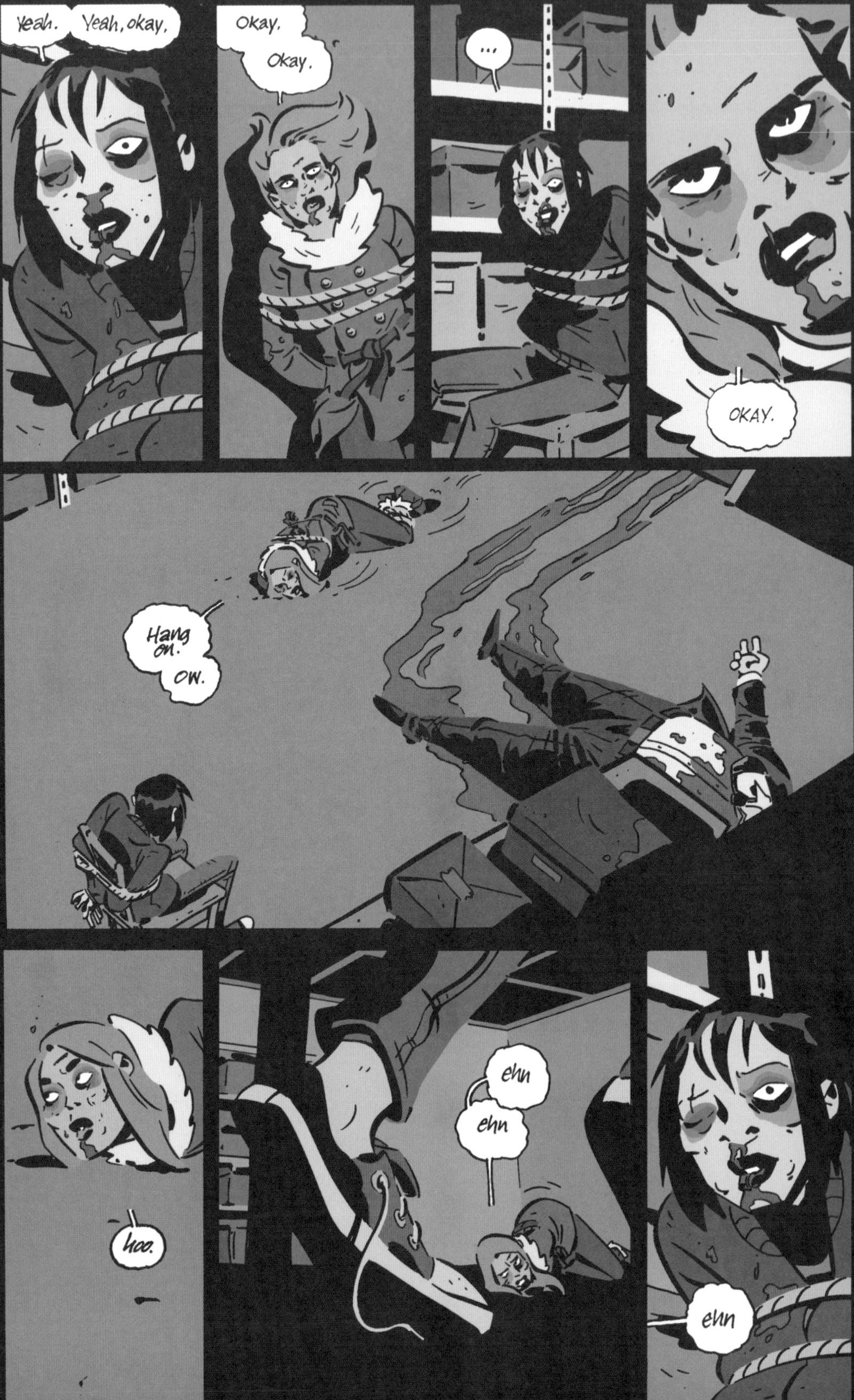
Yeah.
Yeah, okay.
Okay.
Okay.
...
OKAY.
Hang on.
OW.
hoo.
ehn
ehn
ehn

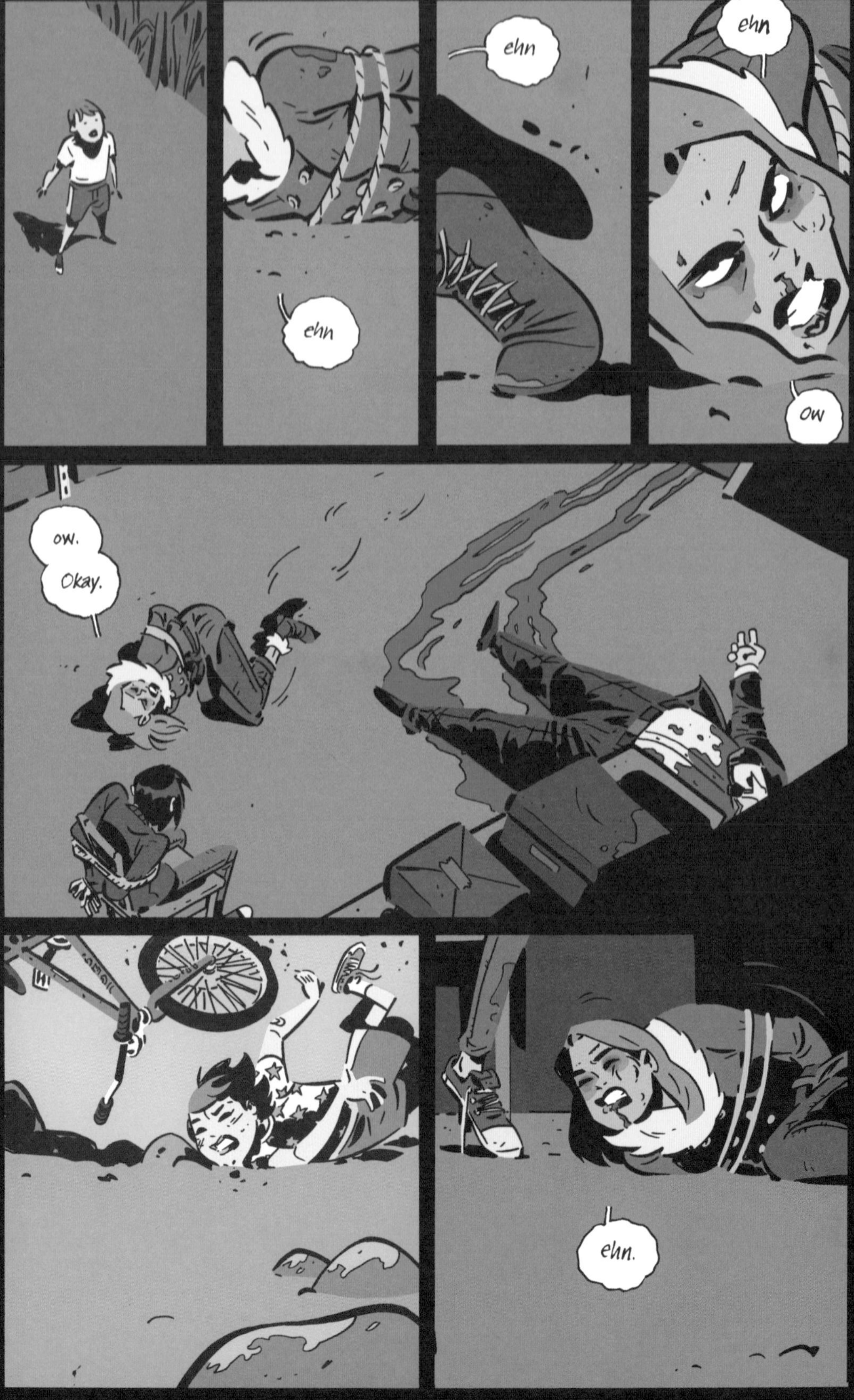
ehn
ehn
ehn
ow
ow.
Okay.
ehn.

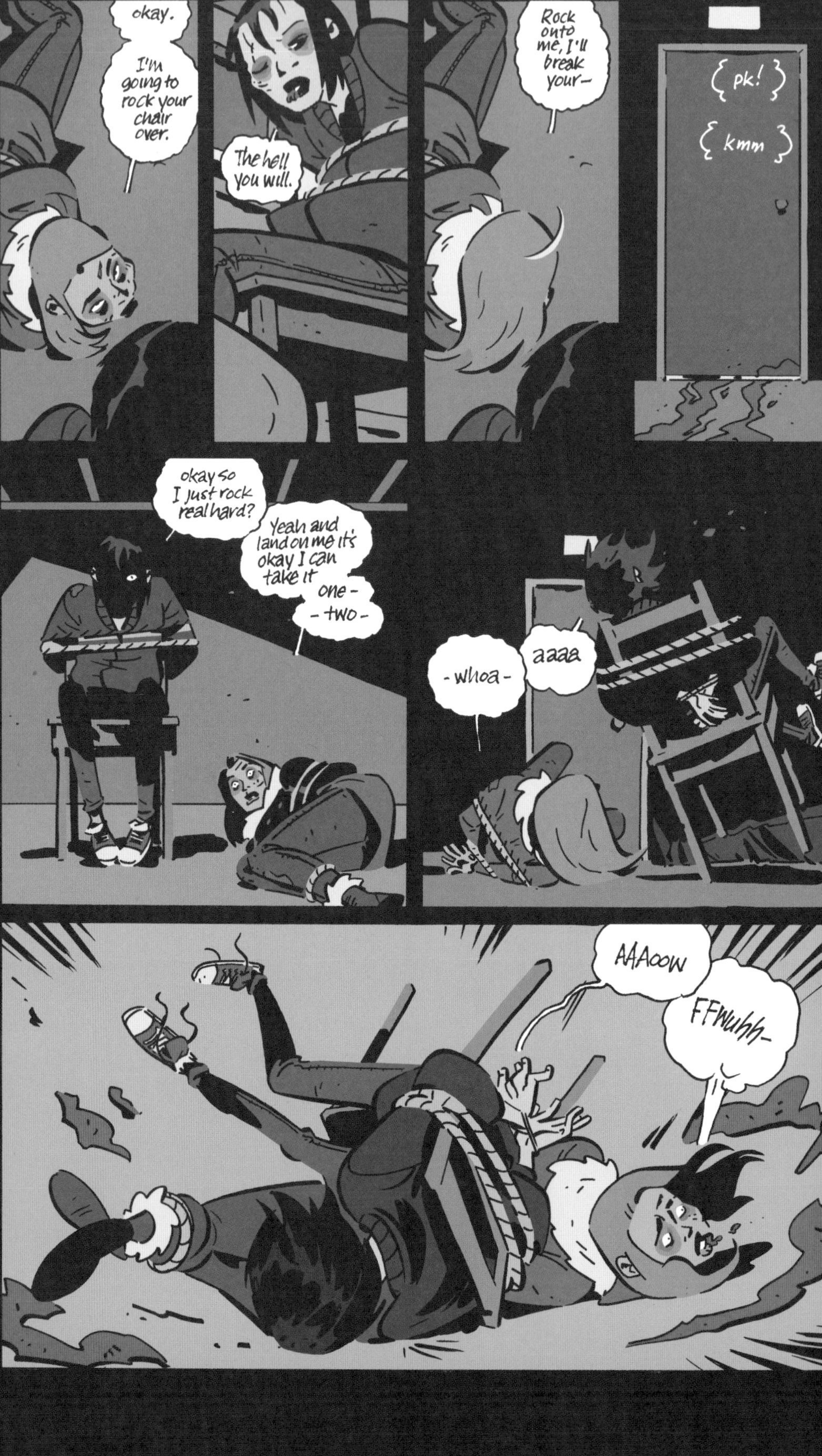
okay.
I'm going to rock your chair over.
The hell you will.
Rock onto me, I'll break your—
{ pk! }
{ kmm }
okay so I just rock real hard?
Yeah and land on me it's okay I can take it
one -
- two -
- whoa -
aaaa
AAAoow
FFWuhh-

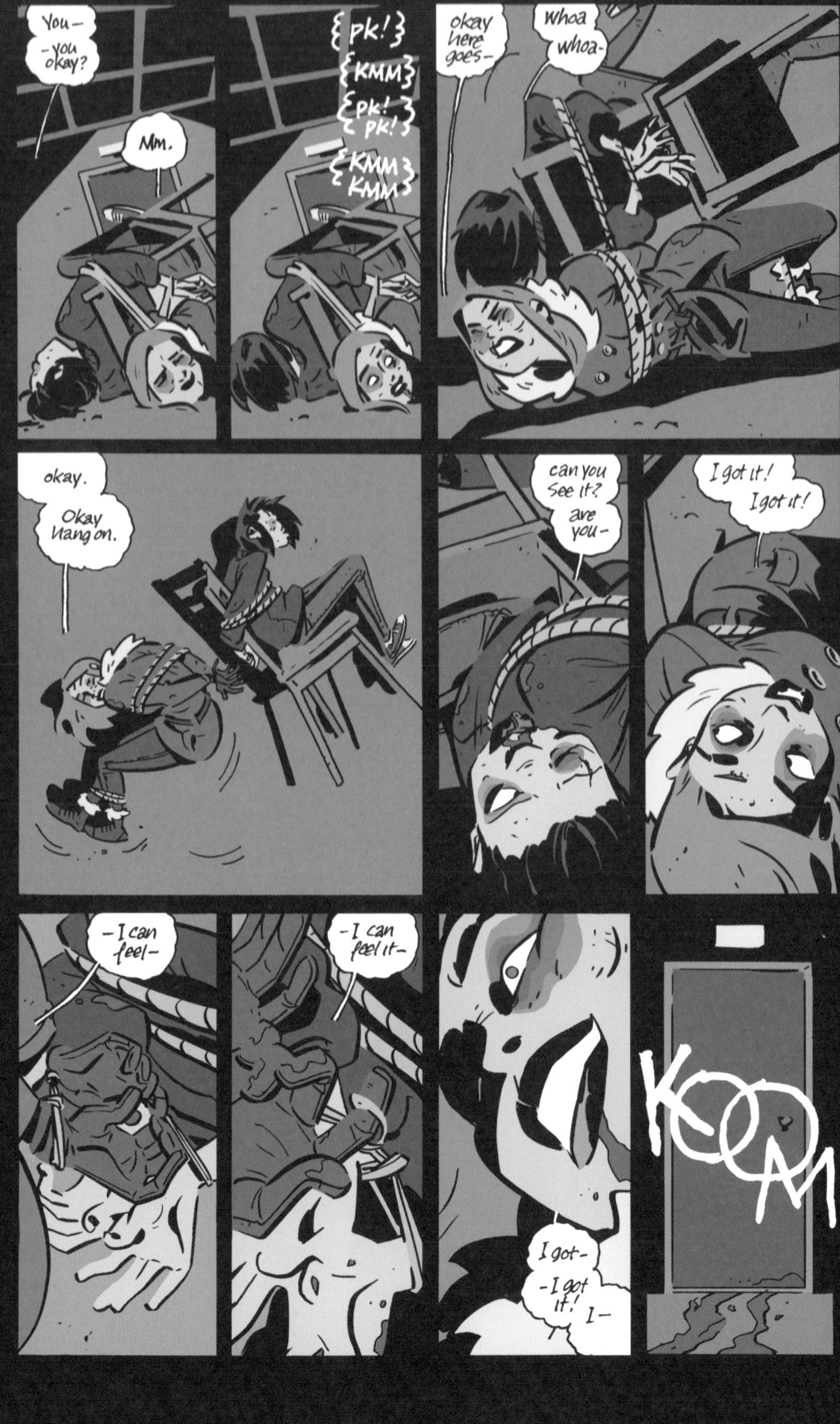
You—
—you okay?
Mm.
{pk!}
{KMM}
{pk! pk!}
{KMM KMM}
okay here goes—
whoa whoa—
okay.
Okay hang on.
can you see it? are you—
I got it! I got it!
—I can feel—
—I can feel it—
I got—
—I got it! I—
KOOM

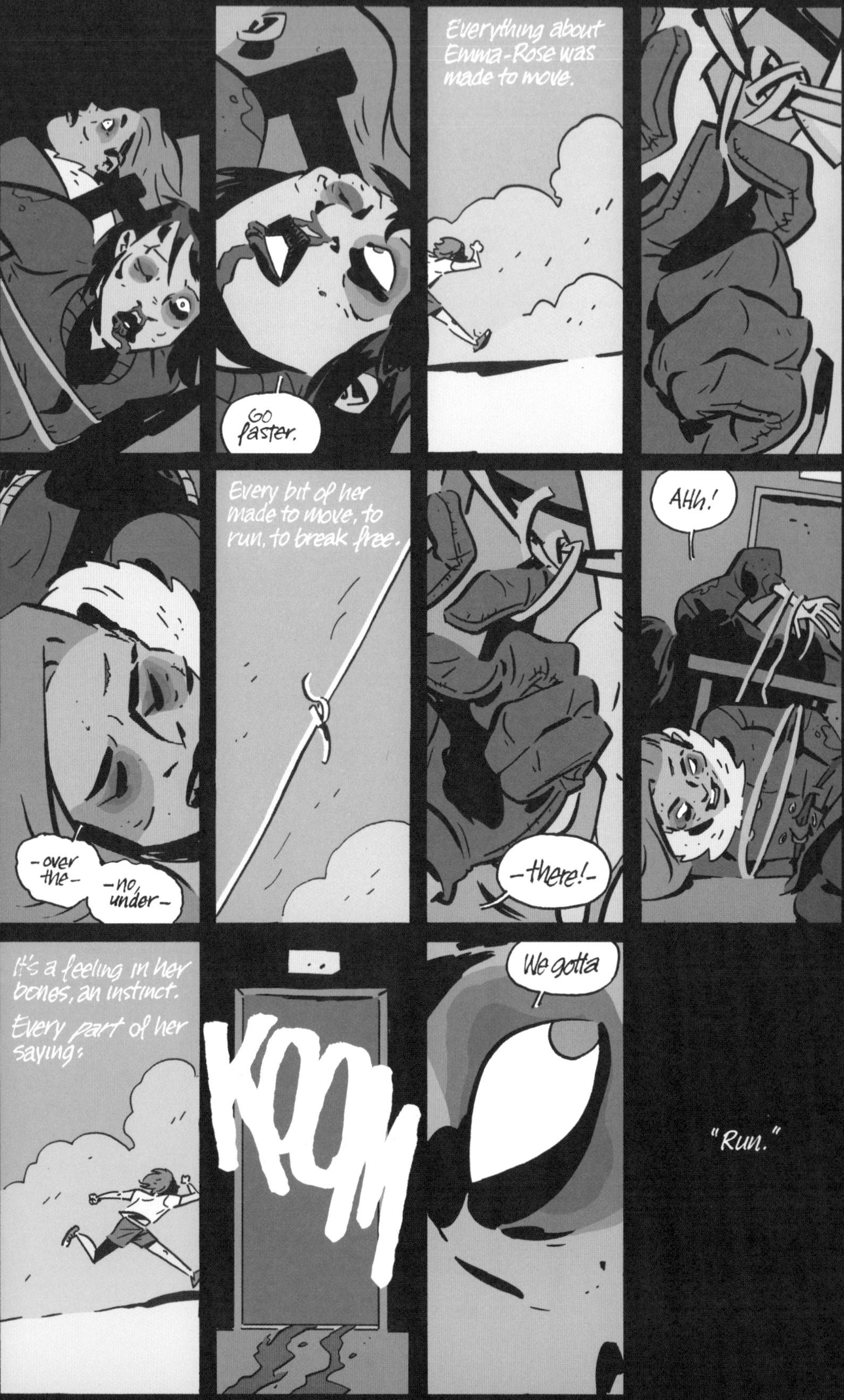
Go faster.
Everything about Emma-Rose was made to move.
-over the-
-no, under-
Every bit of her made to move, to run, to break free.
-there!-
AHh!
It's a feeling in her bones, an instinct.
Every part of her saying:
KOOM
We gotta
"Run."

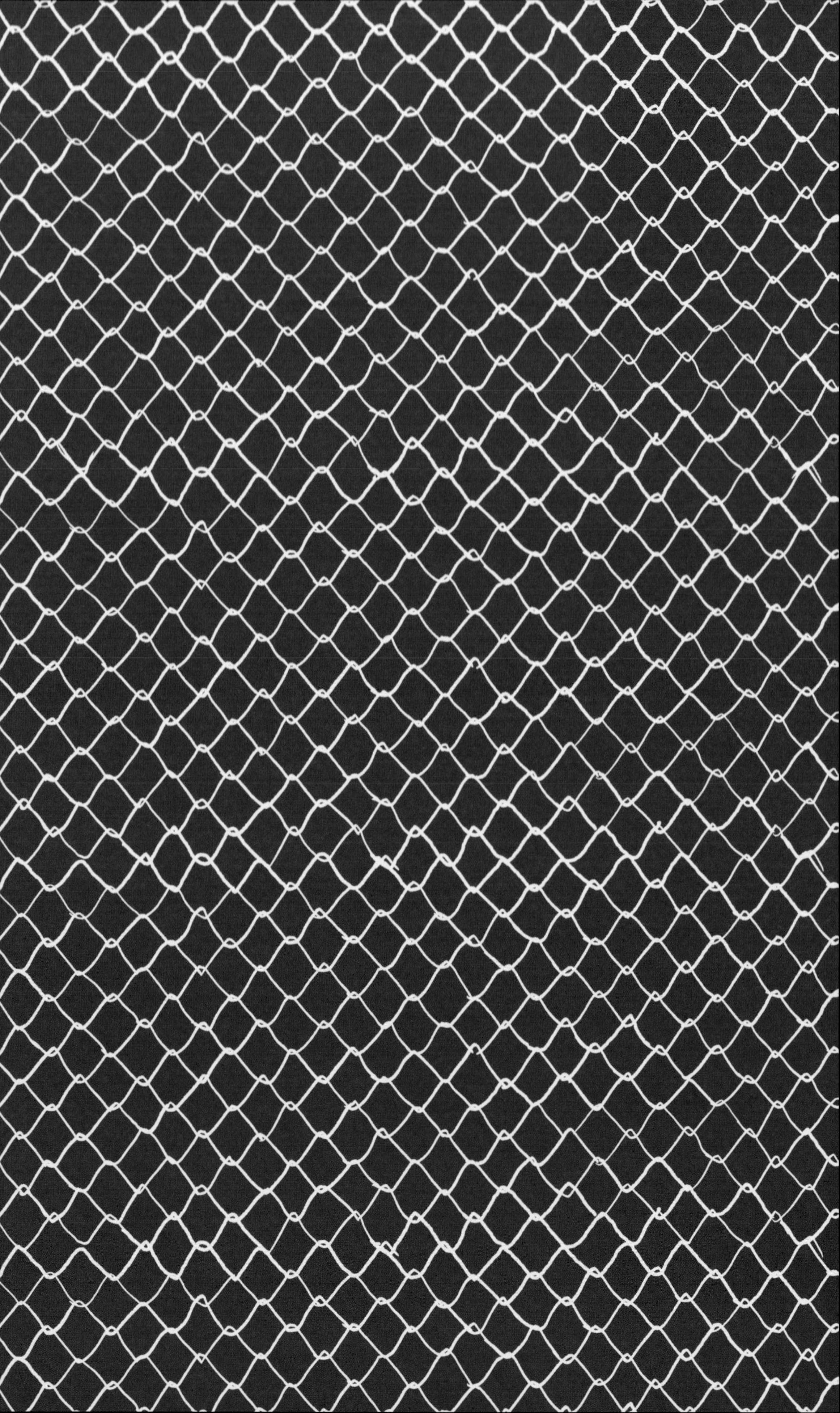

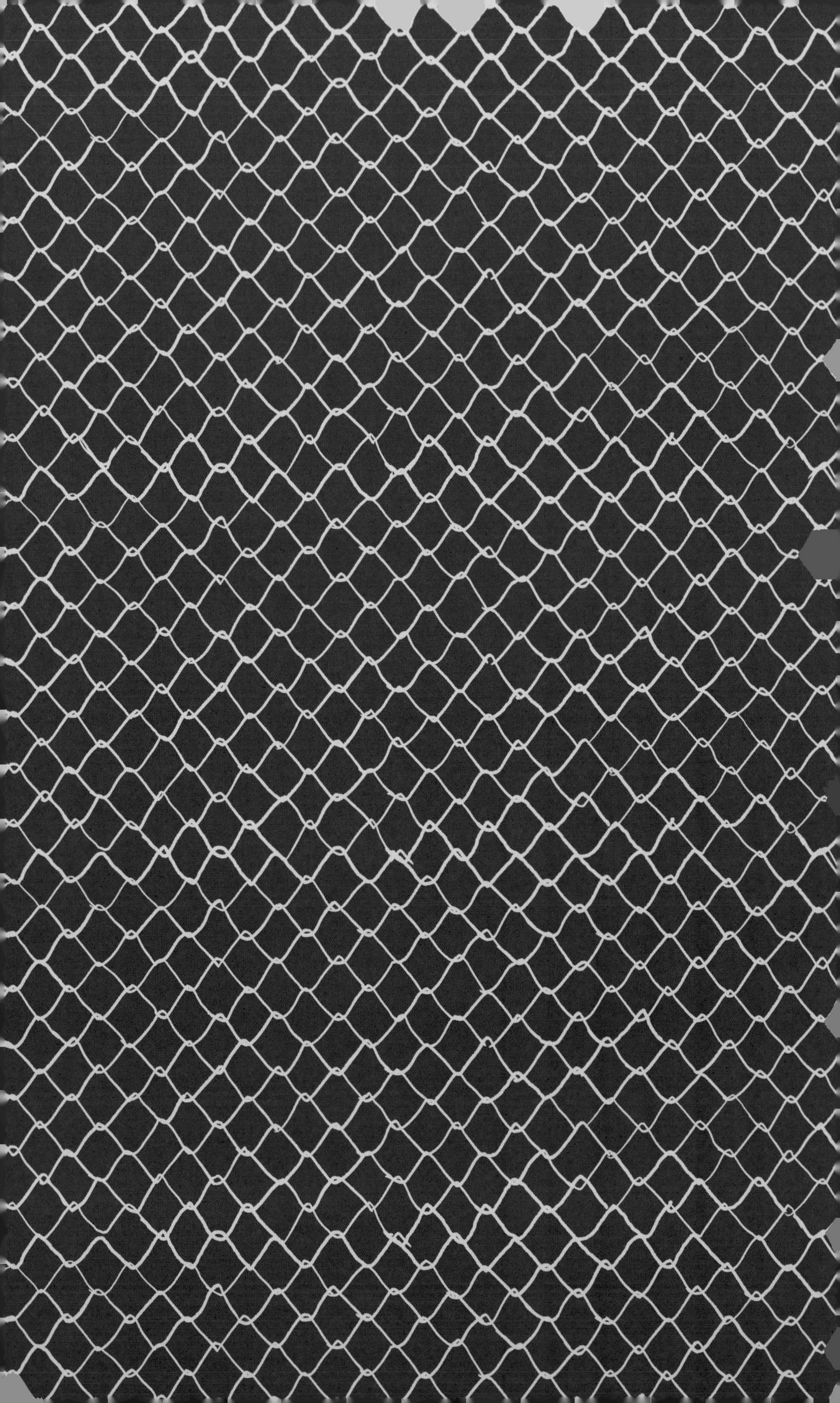

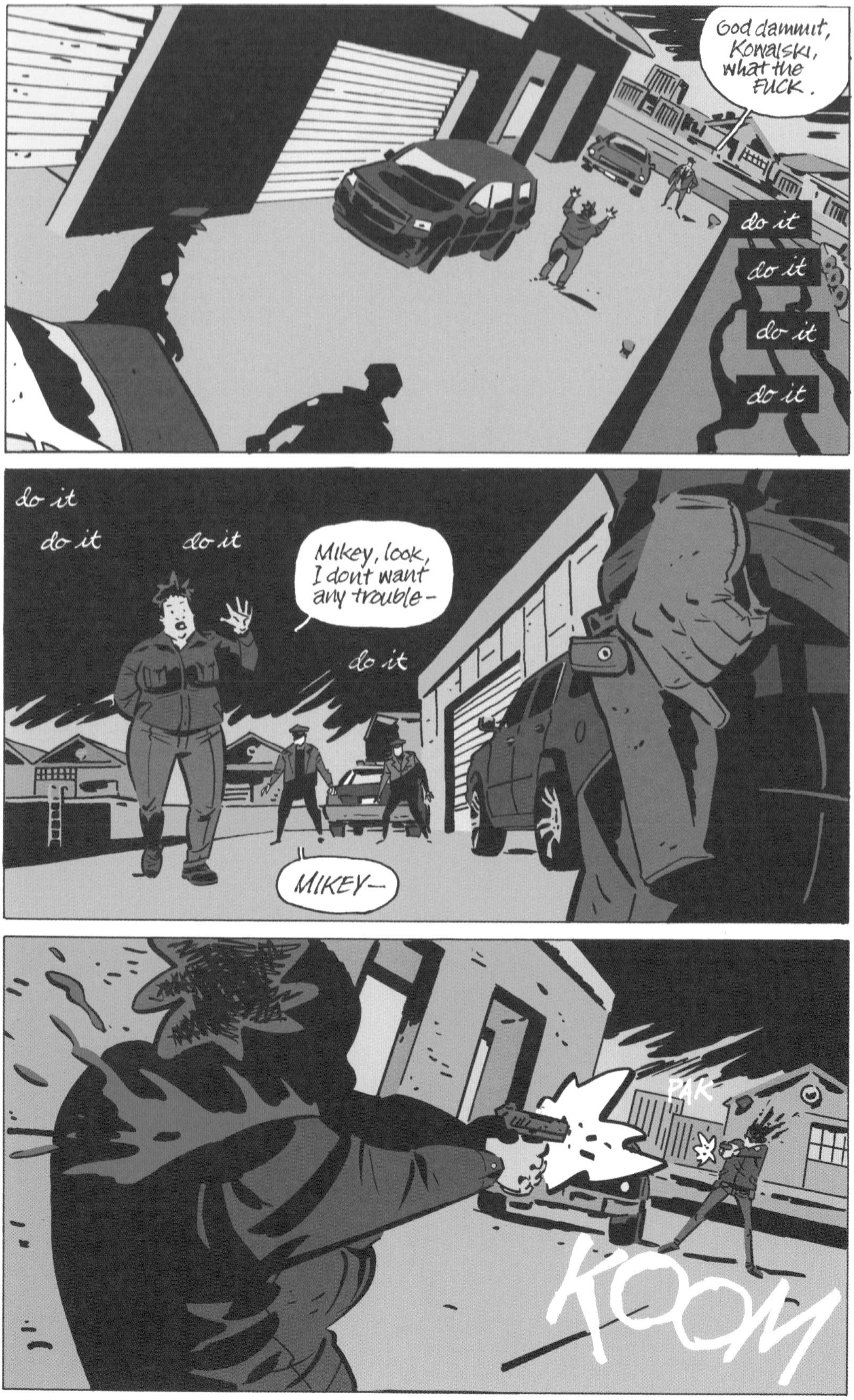
God dammit, Kowalski, what the FUCK.
do it
do it
do it
do it
do it
do it
do it
Mikey, look, I dont want any trouble-
do it
MIKEY-
PAK
KOOM

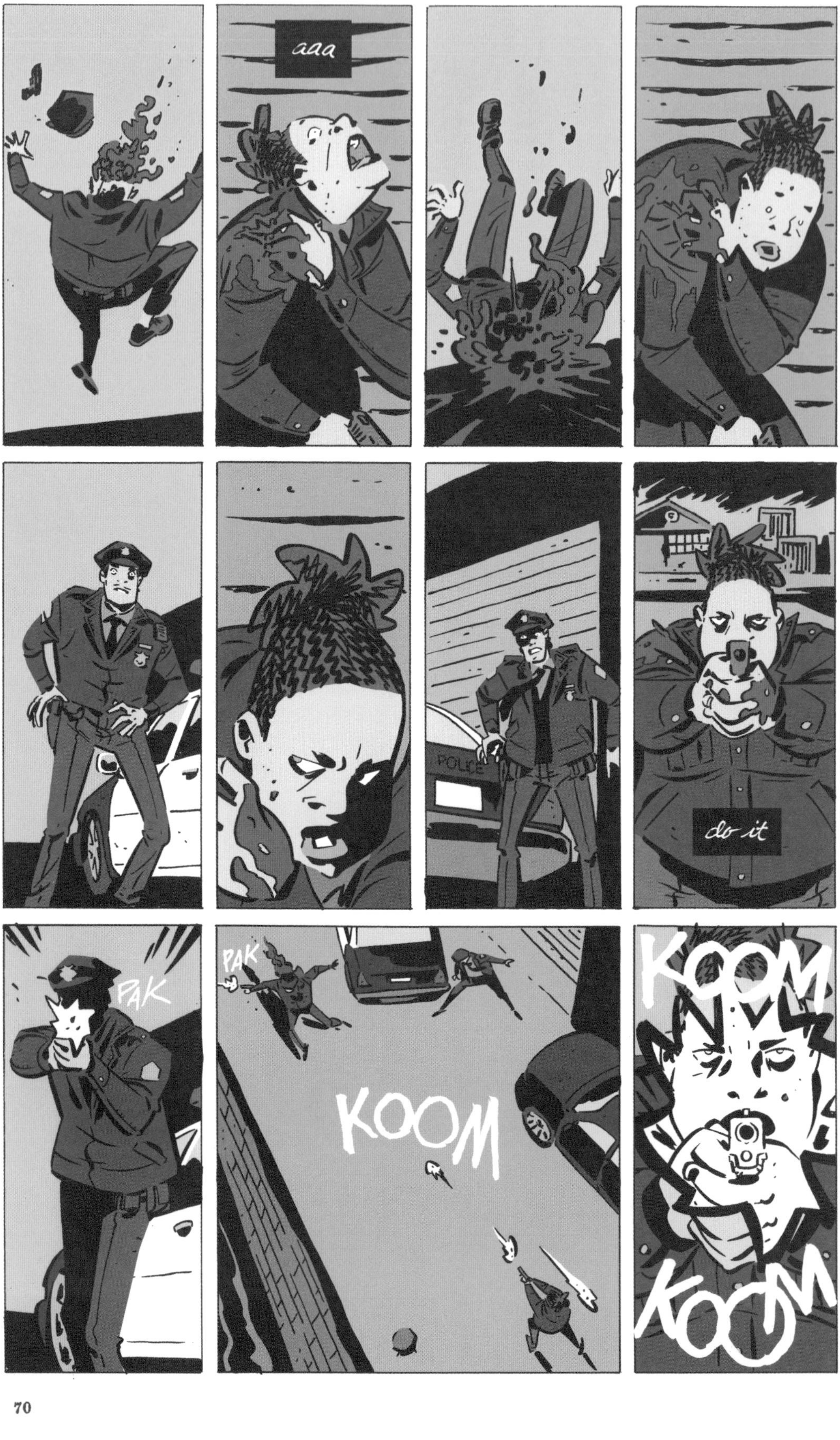
aaa
do it
PAK
PAK
KOOM
KOOM
KOOM

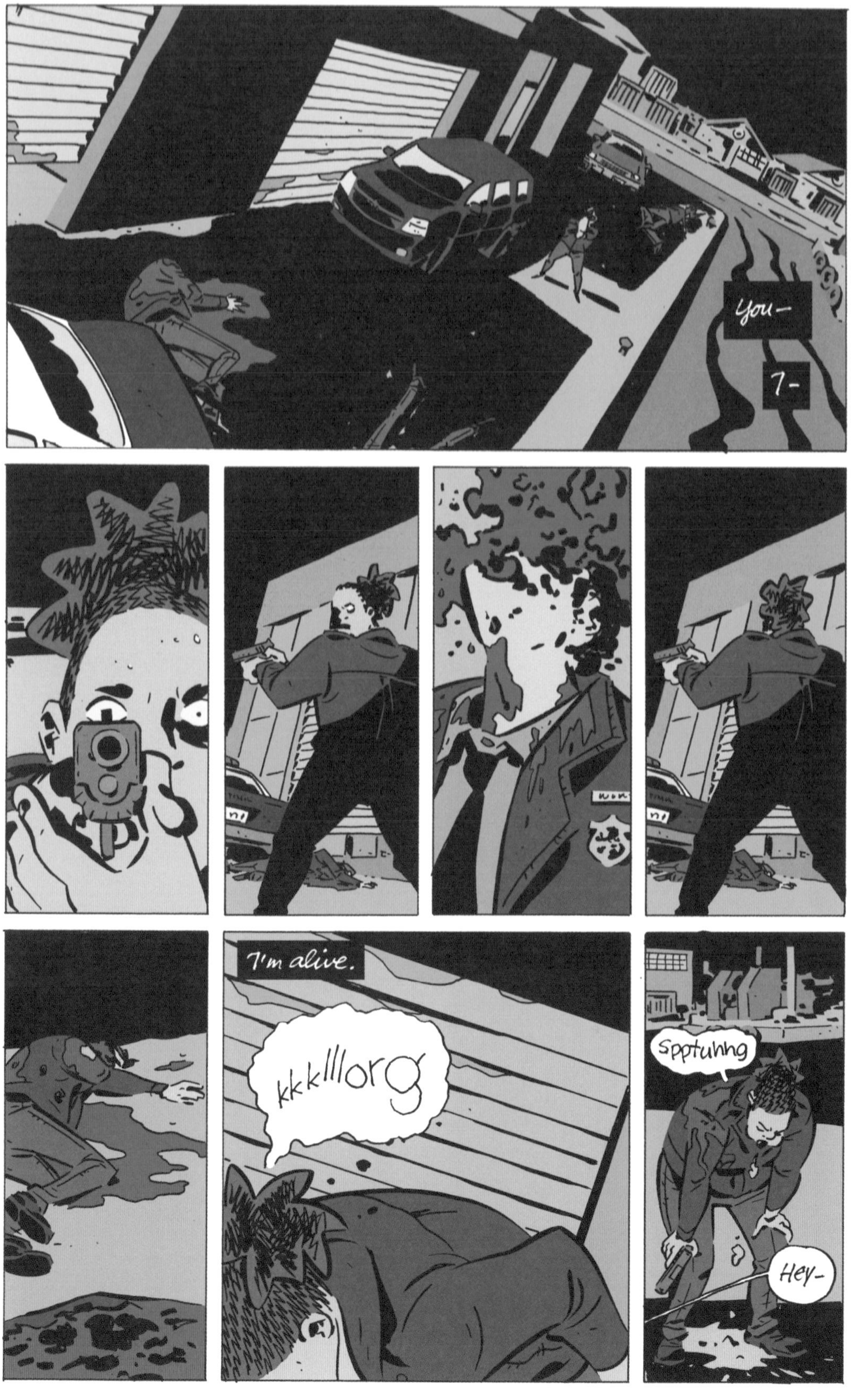
You—
I—
I'm alive.
kkklllorg
Sspptuhng
Hey—

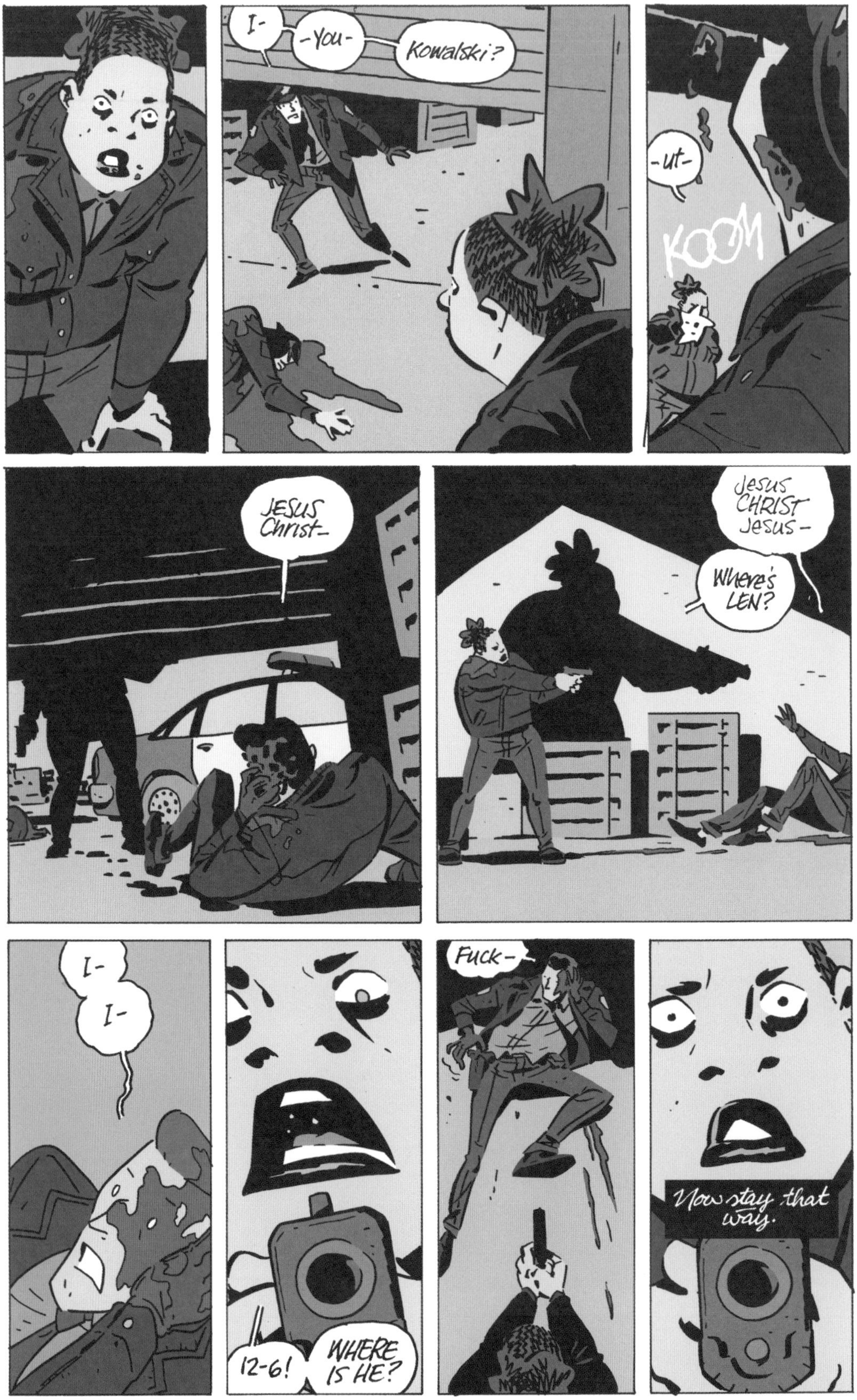
I-
-You-
Kowalski?
-ut-
KOOM
JESUS Christ-
Jesus CHRIST Jesus-
Where's LEN?
I-
I-
12-6!
WHERE IS HE?
Fuck-
Now stay that way.

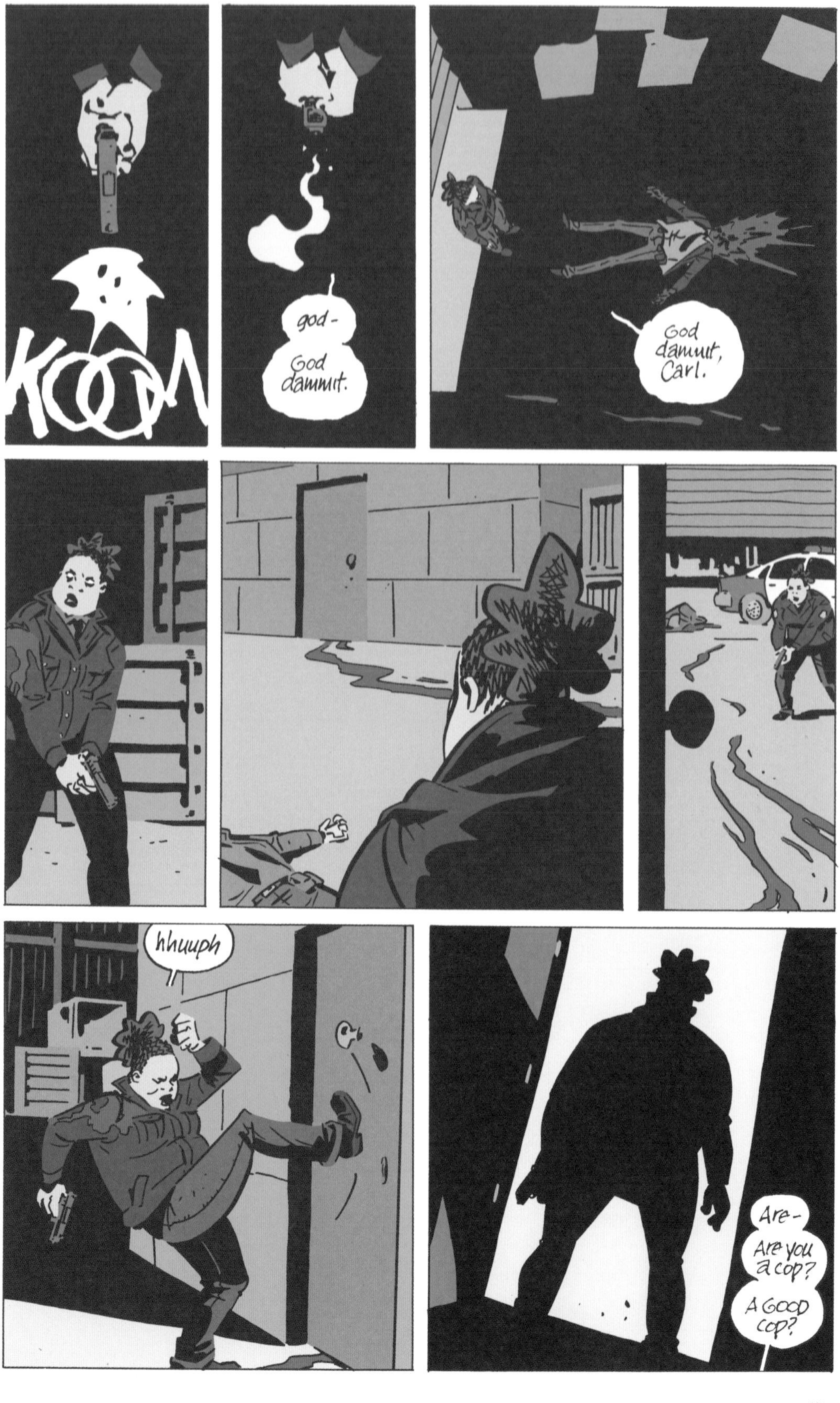
KOOM
god-
God dammit.
God dammit, Carl.
hhuuph
Are-
Are you a cop?
A GOOD cop?

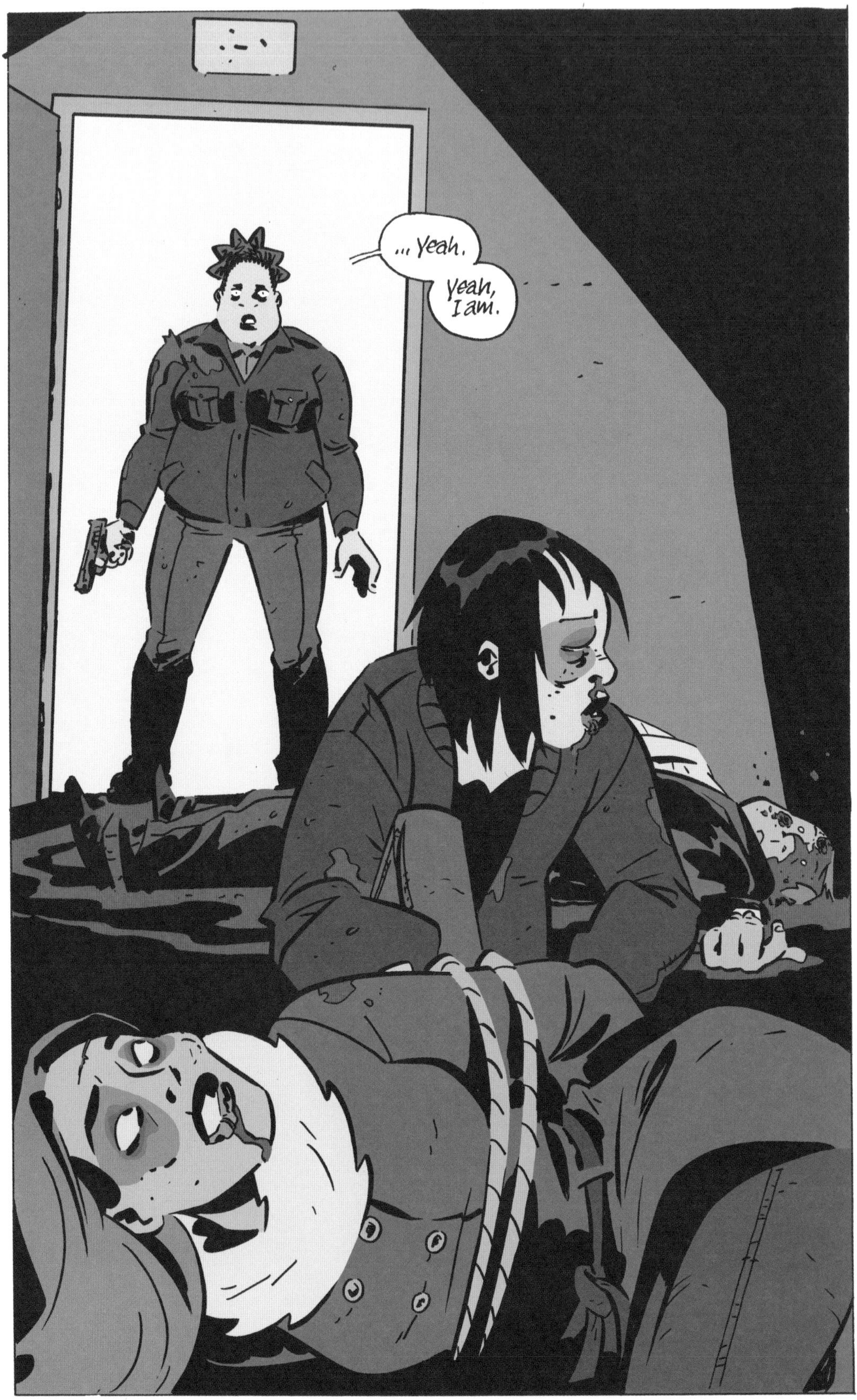
...Yeah.
Yeah, I am.

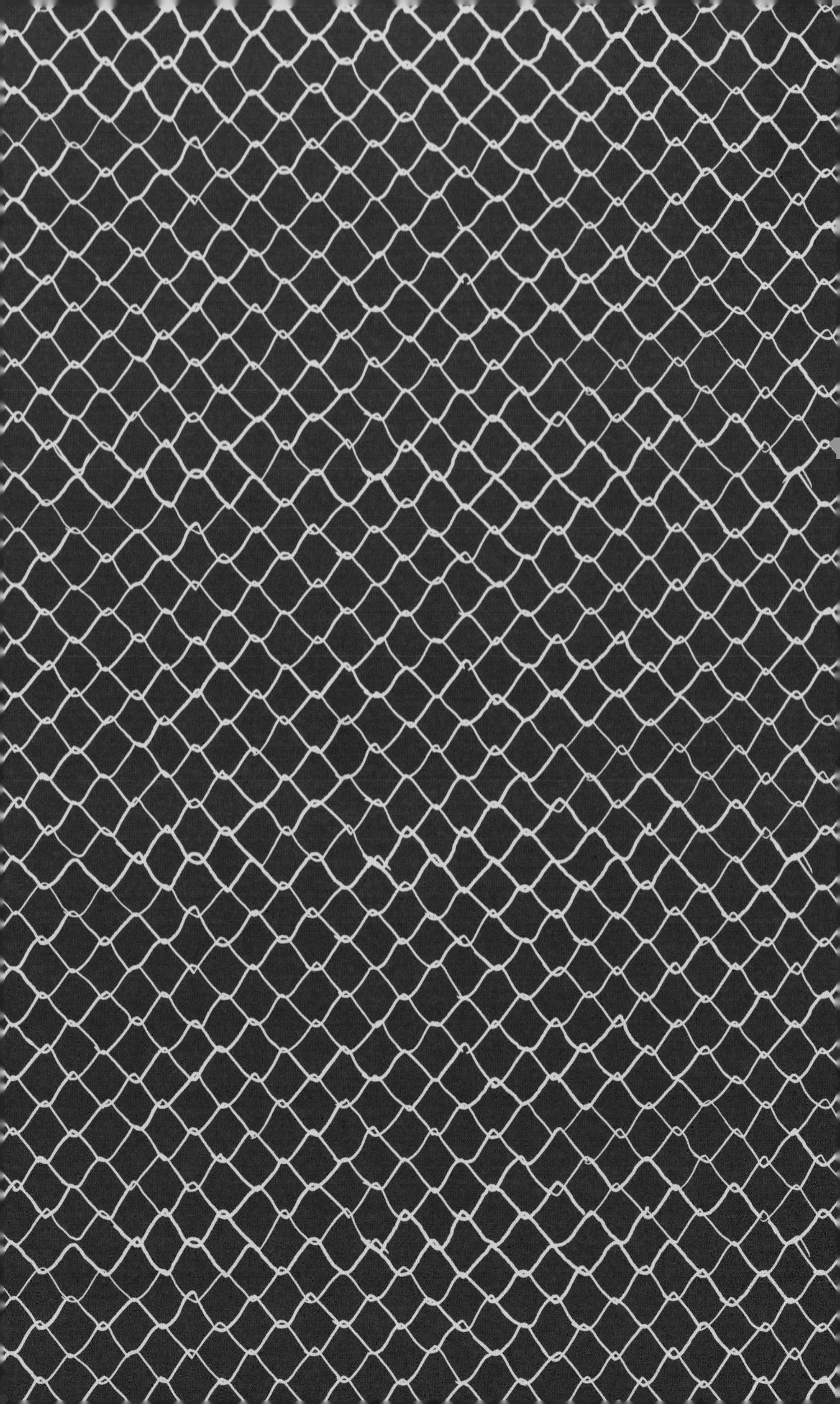

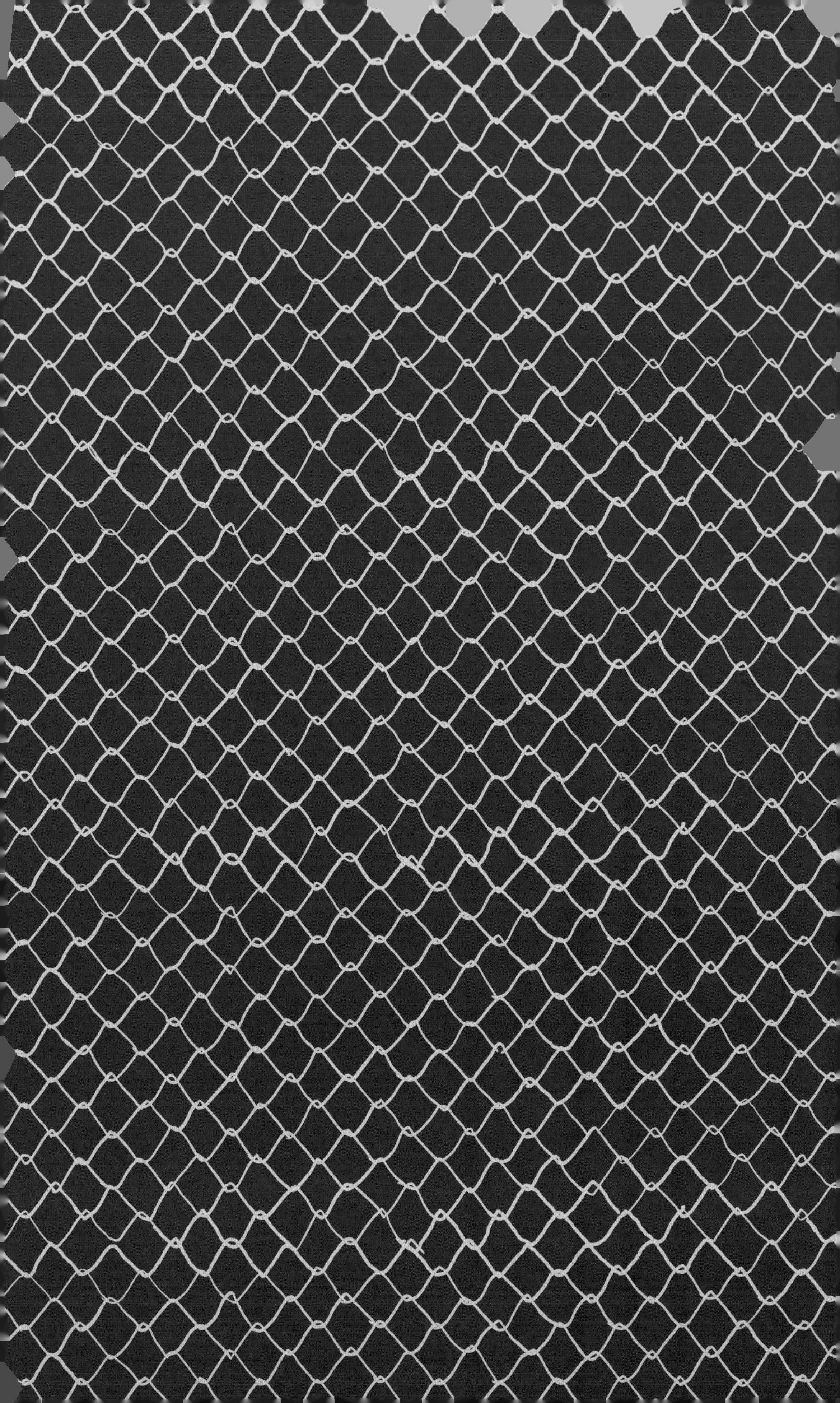

MATT FRACTION
WRITER

ELSA CHARRETIER
ARTIST

MATT HOLLINGSWORTH
COLORIST

KURT ANKENY
LETTERER

RIAN HUGHES
DESIGNER

DEANNA PHELPS
PRODUCTION

TURNER LOBEY
EDITOR

NOVEMBER CREATED BY
MATT FRACTION AND ELSA CHARRETIER

MATT FRACTION writes comic books out in the woods and lives with his wife, writer Kelly Sue DeConnick, his two children, two dogs, a cat, a bearded dragon, and a yard full of coyotes and crows. Surely there's a metaphor there. He's a New York Times bestselling donkus of comics like SEX CRIMINALS (winner of the 2014 Will Eisner Award for Best New Series and named TIME Magazine's Best Comic of 2013), ODY-C, and CASANOVA. Fraction and DeConnick are currently developing television for Legendary TV under their company Milkfed Criminal Masterminds, Inc.

ELSA CHARRETIER is a writer and comic book artist. After debuting on COWL at Image Comics, Elsa co-created THE INFINITE LOOP with writer Pierrick Colinet at IDW. She has since worked at DC Comics (STARFIRE, BOMBSHELLS, HARLEY QUINN), Marvel Comics (THE UNSTOPPABLE WASP), and Random House (WINDHAVEN, written by George R.R. Martin). She has also written THE INFINITE LOOP vol. 2 as well as SUPERFREAKS, and is a regular artist on STAR WARS comic books.

MATT HOLLINGSWORTH has been coloring comics professionally since 1991 and has worked on titles such as PREACHER, WYTCHES, HAWKEYE, DAREDEVIL, HELLBOY, CATWOMAN, THOR, THE FILTH, WOLVERINE, and PUNISHER, among others. He's currently working on BATMAN: CURSE OF THE WHITE KNIGHT for DC Comics as well as SEVEN TO ETERNITY and NOVEMBER for Image Comics. He's won more awards for the beers he's brewed than for the comics he's colored.

KURT ANKENY is an award-winning cartoonist and painter whose work has appeared in Best American Comics, the Society of Illustrators, the Cape Ann Museum, Comics Workbook, Ink Brick, PEN America's Illustrated PEN, and Fantagraphics's NOW anthology. He lives with his wife and son in Salem, Massachusetts.

RIAN HUGHES is a graphic designer, illustrator, comic artist, writer, and typographer who has written and drawn comics for 2000AD and BATMAN: BLACK AND WHITE, and designed logos for James Bond, the X-Men, Superman, Hed Kandi and The Avengers.
His comic strips have been collected in Yesterday's Tomorrows and Tales from Beyond Science, and his burlesque portraits in Soho Dives, Soho Divas. The recent Logo a Gogo collects many of his logo designs for the comic book world and beyond.

IMAGE COMICS, INC.
Robert Kirkman : Chief Operating Officer
Erik Larsen : Chief Financial Officer
Todd McFarlane : President
Marc Silvestri : Chief Executive Officer
Jim Valentino : Vice President
Eric Stephenson : Publisher/Chief Creative Officer
Jeff Boison : Director of Sales & Publishing Planning
Jeff Stang : Director of Direct Market Sales
Kat Salazar : Director of PR & Marketing
Drew Gill : Cover Editor
Heather Doornink : Production Director
Nicole Lapalme : Controller
IMAGECOMICS.COM

NOVEMBER, VOL.3.
First printing.
October 2020
Published by Image Comics, Inc.
Office of publication : 2701 NW Vaughn St., Suite 780,
Portland, OR 97210.

For international rights,
Contact : foreignlicensing@imagecomics.com.
ISBN : 978·1·5343·1602·7

NEXT:
THE MESS WE'RE IN